AF226333

The Journals of Professor Guthridge

THE JOURNALS OF PROFESSOR GUTHRIDGE

KYT WRIGHT

Copyright © 2020 Kyt Wright.

No part of this publication may be reproduced, stored in a retrieval system, or transmitted in any form or by any means, electronic, mechanical, photocopying, recording, or otherwise, without written permission of the publisher.

All rights reserved including the right of reproduction in whole or in part in any form. The moral right of the author has been asserted.

This is a work of fiction. Names, characters, businesses, places, events, locales, and incidents are either the products of the author's imagination or used in a fictitious manner. Any resemblance to actual persons, living or dead, or actual events is purely coincidental.

BLKDOG

www.blkdogpublishing.com

Other titles by Kyt Wright

Sirkkusaga

Love Bites

Chapter One – The Devil Stone

The Journal of Professor Arnold Guthridge, St Aidan's College

October 30th. 1899

No one knows who erected the Devil Stone or why, one local myth says that in days long gone, young women, hoping for a child would pour honey or place a garland of flowers over the *beak* of the column while others hinted at a far darker past, saying the protuberance acted as both anchor point and anvil to strike off the hands or even the head of an unlucky sacrifice tied there. Some said it was called the Devil Stone because it was a signpost for Hell itself and it was told that the screams of its suffering occupants could oft be heard, most especially upon All Hallows Eve. Local folk all agreed it was a place steeped in mystery and best avoided after dark.

So it is with this in mind that I, Professor Arnold Guthridge of St Aidan's College set off to keep all-night vigil and study this so-called haunted stone accompanied by Mr. John Stack, one of my most promising students and his fiancée Mary with her aunt Miss Evelyn Poole (a lec-

"

turer in Ancient Languages at Winterton college for ladies, no less!) as chaperone.

October 31st 6.30 pm; after making a fire some distance from the stone we settled down for the night. John had brought his camera and had set it up on a tripod with the intent of taking regular photographs, we had with us a pair of the new battery-powered torches (they are notoriously unreliable so we have also brought some good old bullseye oil lanterns). The ladies are both scared and excited in equal measure, Aunt Evelyn is pretending not to be affected thus but it is quite apparent to me so John and I have assured them that they will come to no harm with us here.

8.30 pm; Mary insisted she saw something moving in the trees ahead of the stone, I valiantly went to investigate and I freely admit to it, almost jumped out of my skin when a fox ran out of the undergrowth. I returned to much laughter and we boiled up a kettle to have tea and partake of the delicious "Scottish" shortbread her aunt had brought and I must admit the spinster has a fine cast to her face.

9.00 pm; a strange drowsiness has overcome the party, Mary has fallen asleep on John's lap and after finally running out of conversation Evelyn and I sat together against a tree to doze.

11.00 pm; an unholy sound woke us all with a start; it could be best described as the deep sonorous unending toll of a large bell deep underground. Evelyn, who had fallen into my arms as we slept, gave me a guilty look before rushing to comfort her niece who was quite shaken by the noise. Then it stopped suddenly as if cut off so I assisted my student in taking a few photographs using flash powder, we all even stood bravely before the stone pillar with John operating the camera at distance with a squeeze bulb and never had waiting for the correct exposure taken so long.

12.00; midnight, I am writing this after the terrible event so please forgive me if I have missed something out. I must have fallen into a swoon for when I came round I was shocked to see Mary, clad only in her bodice and under-skirts moving and pressing herself against the stone pillar in a most unladylike way as John and her Aunt both seemingly in a daze, were busily binding her hands to the beak-like protuberance. Imagine my horror when I observed spectral figures dancing around them and though I could not clearly make out their appearance I saw several were carrying scythes and axes! Producing the pistol I had concealed in my jacket I fired it into the air crying. "You must stop this madness now!"

This had the effect of bringing all to their senses and while Evelyn covered Mary's modesty her fiancé hastily unfastened her bindings, the figures, now aware of my presence glared at me malevolently and began to approach. I aimed my gun but realising it would be useless against such ethereal creatures went quickly to my bag to produce an electric torch and shine it upon them, I knew not why I knew it would work but the eldritch forms shied away from the bright light. Evelyn and Mary ran to our camp and I threw the other torch to John who upon catching it drove the things back further.

"Come on man let us flee while we can!" I cried, for the primitive hiding inside this man of science realised flight was the best action but John had found a large rock and was smashing it down upon the *beak* intending to destroy it. "Professor, keep your light upon me for it will halt their approach" he yelled.

Evelyn had acquired a lantern and lighting it joined me to shine her beam, wan by comparison to my electric light, on him. Then just as he chipped off a massive piece the torch failed, leaving only the bullseye barely illuminating the proceedings. A ghastly scream rang out and with no attempt at valour all three of us fled leaving everything behind including Mary's poor swain…

November 1st; I returned the next day with a pair of local constables and several sturdy yeomen to discover the protuberance broken from the pillar to lay in pieces on the earth.

"You shouldn't have meddled!" exclaimed one of the locals upon seeing it.

Another nodded sagely. "No-one sensible comes here after dusk and 'tis better for you that you never come here again, they're going to be plenty angry now."

I recovered our things while the rest of the party searched the area thoroughly, but of John Stack could be found no sign ...

November 4th; once safely back at the university I had the photographic plates developed inviting Evelyn (who had proved herself a sturdy individual and with whom I have developed quite an affinity) to examine them with me, leaving Mary safely ensconced with her parents and grieving for her lost love. Lighting the projector's lamp I closed the curtains and we viewed John's handiwork, rapidly changing the slides which displayed nothing other than various exposures of the pillar, now a source of abhorrence to us both, until we reached the last slide showing our party stood before the cursed thing.

I cannot easily describe what we saw on the slide, I don't have the words but Evelyn grabbed my hand in the dark to squeeze it tightly. "Arnold, they didn't want my niece, she merely whetted their appetite" she whispered in shock.

I had to admit the lady was right, for there visible on the slide, indescribable monstrosities gathered about us. For some reason they chose to ignore Evelyn and I completely and though a scant few hovered by Mary the majority were gathered around, staring intently, eagerly and one might almost say hungrily, at my poor student John...

A. Guthridge (Professor of Arcane Studies, St Aidan's)

Chapter Two – Mary Brings News

The young woman rang the bell then peered through the frosted glass in the door's small window to see a figure in red approaching.

"Why Mary this is a surprise!" said the figure upon opening it, a smoky incense issuing from within.

"I bring exciting news Aunt Evie," announced Mary Poole curiously regarding her aunt, who appeared to be clad in only a loose brightly coloured oriental robe.

Evelyn, spotting her niece's attention, pulled the robe close to her to explain guiltily. "I was meditating my dear. Make yourself at home in the parlour while I put on something more appropriate."

Mary wandered into the comfortably furnished room to sit in a large chair and while waiting for her aunt picked up a book from the low table there. She began idly leafing through the tome which was lavishly illustrated with depictions of...

"Oh!" the young woman exclaimed aloud, her eyes widening.

"It's a translation of a treatise on Tantric Worship" her aunt, now properly attired, enlightened her as she returned to the room.

"But Auntie surely you have never indulged in such practices?"

"Mary, you are only just twenty and have much to learn," replied Evelyn, a smile upon her face.

"I could never do such things!" retorted her niece.

Evelyn laughed lightly. "We'll see, now let me hear your exciting news."

"Aunt Evie, I am once again engaged to be married," stated Mary, putting the book down as though it would bite her.

"That is indeed good news and I must declare somewhat of a surprise. May I ask who the lucky gentleman is?"

"Lord William Theddingworth, he proposed to me only the other day."

"But I didn't even know you were walking out with anyone, let alone courtship?"

"I was reluctant to mention it after that business with poor John."

"Well, it has been over a year now Mary and you are only human when all is said and done." Evelyn thought for a while. "I have heard of this man and as I recall he's somewhat older than you isn't he, closer to my age I believe?"

"Love acknowledges no age limits Auntie and besides isn't Professor Guthridge more than ten years older than you?" Mary referred to her aunt's unconventional relationship with the respected Professor of Arcane Studies of St Aidan's College.

"Touché Mary," replied Evelyn lightly. "Of course I shall want to meet your suitor."

"Naturally, father has already given his approval but I do value your good opinion."

My brother is a poor judge of character and his wife no better, thought Evelyn before declaring aloud. "Then you must arrange a meeting for me with your esteemed beau."

Chapter Three – Lord William's Secret

So it was that a few days later Evelyn found herself at Pendleberry Hall, the majestic ancestral home of the Theddingworth family. She had done a little research into the man's ancestry using a well-known tome of the Peerage kept in St Aidan's library and the family seemed quite unremarkable, the prevalence of the name William coming into vogue a little over a hundred years previously with the first owner of that name. A man who had travelled widely in Bohemia and eastern Europe.

Evelyn had journeyed up from Oxford by train with Mary and her parents, her older brother Vivian who had a position in the Civil Service and his wife Cecilia. He was genial and somewhat over trusting, not the dynamic man their father had been, while his wife, quiet and demure was Evelyn's diametric opposite.

Pendleberry Hall was a magnificent edifice that screamed affluence and Evelyn had to concede that Mary had done very well for herself, *if he lives up to expectations that is!* The tall doors were opened by an ageing butler, who led them to a study overflowing with taxidermy and antiquities where the master of the house stood by the fireplace.

Lord William introduced himself greeting them all warmly and Evelyn could understand why her niece had been so smitten, he possessed an athletic physique, was of a handsome mien with fair wavy hair and a large handlebar moustache. "And you can only be Aunt Evelyn" stated the fine-looking man turning to Evie and kissing her out-stretched hand rather than shaking it. "Why, Mary's description of you hardly does you credit."

"Thank you, sir, I believe you flatter me unnecessari-ly," she replied, feeling somewhat warm inside.

"Nonsense, it seems that all the ladies of this family are outstanding though I have to confess Mary is by far the loveliest. Please follow me to the main reception room which is more convivial and we will take tea."

It had been a long journey which would necessitate an overnight stay and as they followed their host, Mary turned to Evelyn to ask. "Well, what do you think, Auntie, is he not just the most perfect man?"

"I've only just met him dear child, but I cannot argue that he is most handsome and charming" she replied, *perhaps a little too charming?*

Mary had met her intended only a month ago. She had been invited with her parents to a fashionable soiree attended by Mrs. Alice Keppel, who was on the arm of a man looking remarkably like the former Prince of Wales. Lord William had approached Evelyn's niece and she found herself uncommonly entranced by his good looks and polite manner. After courting her for only a few weeks he had proposed and she accepted without a moment's hesitation.

They spent the rest of the afternoon in pleasant con-versation then after dinner their host took them once again into the study to show off the collection of ephemera he had garnered from all corners of the globe. Evelyn found them most fascinating, questioning him on some of the more outlandish idols and fetishes in his possession and

Lord William, impressed by her knowledge complimented her greatly causing no small amount of chagrin in her niece. The evening was completed by a round of Bridge with William and Mary versus Evelyn and Cecilia while Vivian was content to sit reading by the fire and indulging himself in the lord's brandy before they all retired to bed.

As Evelyn drifted off to sleep a feeling of concern ran through her mind, there was something about Lord William's manner that she could not put a finger on.

He seemed too good to be true.

Something started Evelyn from slumber and she sat up quickly to see the man himself stood by her bedside. "What do you want?" she cried in alarm, pulling up the bedclothes to cover her modesty, for Evie believed it healthy to sleep *au naturel*.

"Evelyn, you are an incredible woman both in mind and body and I believe most experienced in life?" he appeared very handsome in the light of the candles by her bedside, Evelyn felt drawn into his eyes and found herself imagining being with him in a most physical and intimate sense. Letting the covers slip from her bosom she leaned forward to kiss him as he bent to her.

Their lips touched briefly. "No!" she shouted coming to her senses.

"Quiet!" he hissed grabbing Evelyn by the shoulders but she managed to rake her fingernails down his face to leave long bleeding scratches there and snatched her trusty Webley from under the pillow as he recoiled only to watch in horror as the wounds quickly healed to disappear and leave only a smear of blood on his cheek.

Wiping his face with the back of his hand he addressed her. "Evelyn, I meant you no harm" in response she cocked the revolver to point it at his head. "Go ahead pull the trigger, I can assure you it will not end my sorry life but it will doubtless wake everyone in the house."

"What in God's name are you?" asked Evie, keeping her aim straight and true.

"You are an erudite woman Evelyn, I'm sure you must be familiar with the word vampyr?"

"I have read the stories by Le Fanu and Stoker, are you telling me you are one of these undead creatures?" retorted Evelyn, covering her modesty with the sheets once again.

"Not a vampyr no, over a hundred years ago while travelling in Moldavia I encountered a self-professed scholar of the arcane, an old man who offered to sell me an amount of powdered vampyr blood which would guarantee life eternal to any who consumed it. I scoffed at him, of course, but he insisted he was over a century old himself and suggested I stab him with a knife to prove its healing properties. I refused to do such a thing as any gentleman would, so he cut his own arm severely then bade me watch as it healed almost immediately. I purchased the blood for a vast sum of money and after taking it have lived for these many long years, never ageing, never falling ill and no injury will cause me permanent harm. I possess the mesmeric ability of the vampyr but do not have its thirst for blood, nor am I troubled by daylight or garlic."

"That would explain why you have to disappear and return as your own son, you cannot be seen to live forever!" exclaimed Evelyn.

"I was right about you Evelyn you are a most intelligent woman."

"So why propose to Mary only to try and seduce me?"

"I have lived for over a hundred years watching those who I cared for wither away and die while I cannot. Oh, I have trusted servants and money enough to indulge my every whim but longevity has its drawbacks Evelyn, I am lonely and I want someone to share eternity with. I believed Mary to be the right one until I met you."

"But how could this be possible without vampyr blood?"

"I bought all that the man had and enough remains

to grant eternal life to one other, Evelyn, I am offering you the chance to live with me forever."

Evelyn briefly considered how it would be to spend eternity with this handsome wealthy man then thought of Arnold, who was in truth her soulmate. "No, I cannot accept your offer for I love another but you must tell Mary of your secret!"

"She already knows!" came an angry voice from beyond the open door.

The pair turned and a figure stepped in to be illuminated by the candle's soft glow. "Oh God, Mary, how much of that did you hear?" asked her Aunt.

"Enough!" replied the girl sharply.

* * *

As Evelyn boarded the train to Oxford she turned to her niece who had come to see her off, her parents having remained at their prospective son-in-law's stately pile. "Are you sure you know what you're doing Mary?"

"Yes Auntie quite sure, how often does one get the chance to marry into a fortune and receive eternal life into the bargain?"

"What about his attention towards me, can you trust a man like that?" countered her Aunt.

Mary smiled wryly "A brief aberration on his part I'm sure and don't forget I'm going to be twenty and rich forever. I'll not want for the company of others should I so desire it."

"So you have agreed to imbibe this vampire blood?" asked Evelyn, surprised at her niece's *sangfroid*.

"Auntie, for your information it's too late to ask that question for I went with William to his room that very night and I drank a potion made from the foul tasting stuff!" she flushed. "And I did something else too."

"Something you said you could never do, Mary?" asked Evie with a smile.

Her countenance was bright with embarrassment. "Yes! Oh dear, will you tell your professor, will he write of this in his blessed journal?"

"Do not worry Mary, you may be assured that my lips are sealed" replied her aunt.

"Talking of books, if you could find a copy of that Tantricky thing?" asked Mary sheepishly.

Evelyn smiled knowingly. "I'll send one to you as a wedding present."

Chapter Four – The Blue Crystal

The Journal of Professor Arnold Guthridge, St Aidan's College

Thursday, August 16th 1900.
I have a tale to relate that affects me greatly as it concerns a dear colleague of mine.

Victor Henry Torrence was an antiquarian of great enthusiasm and zeal with an income to match, I had first become acquainted with the man while at university and our mutual fascination with all things arcane made firm friends of us from the beginning. While I pursued the path of academia Victor used his not inconsiderable inheritance to roam the world seeking esoteric knowledge, often bringing curiosities and ephemera back from his travels, several of which are proudly displayed in the library at St Aidan's.

Upon returning from a walking holiday in the Alps with my beloved Evie I discovered a pair of letters from my esteemed friend waiting for me, Victor had recently returned from an expedition to remote Patagonia and in the first described in great detail his encounters with shamans of the indigenous tribes there, who by use of potions containing coca leaves could astrally project to a realm of spirits and rainbow light. He wrote of the large quantities of the mineral pitchblende (or Uranite as it is sometimes known) that lay upon the forest floor for the taking and waxed lyrical and at great length with regard to a large crystal, which seemed to glow with a blue light, discovered while searching a ruined temple. The native shaman became agitated upon seeing him with it urging Victor to cast it down a deep chasm but on realising my friend's determination to return it to England, had warned him to keep it locked in a sturdy container at all times. Victor could be a foolhardy man but sensing the man's concern to be genuine, had a lockable metal case fabricated for it by a local craftsman before leaving the continent with it and suggested that I should come see this marvel for myself. The bulk of the letter was composed of such trivial stuff as shared by old friends and he ended by giving his best wishes to Evelyn, complimenting me on my good fortune in meeting such a remarkable woman.

In the second shorter missive he wondered why I had not replied to his first letter (we were of course in Switzerland at the time of its delivery) and in an attempt to further my interest, wrote at great length of his study of the crystal using scientific methodology. He had subjected it to electrical current and chemical testing and discovered that exposure to its light gave him a great sense of well-being. Several large moles that he had on his body since birth had vanished completely and his skin had taken on a shiny almost new appearance. I became uneasy at this, for I had heard reports of pitchblende causing lesions and changes to the skin followed by a vomiting sickness. Since he had discovered the crystal where the mineral was plentiful might it be tainted somehow?

I was writing to warn Victor against further experimentation when an urgent telegram arrived insisting that I must visit him as soon as possible and that I was to come alone and under no circumstances tell anyone. The very next morning I caught a train to the nearest railway station and a swift carriage ride brought me to Victor's large country house where I found his butler in a state of great consternation for after sending the telegram my friend had locked himself in the small outhouse he used for research and had not emerged since. His man, Soames, informed me that of recent his master had begun to develop an unpleasant pallor with a blue glow seeming to emanate from within his skin when in shadow and the rest of the staff, while fearing for his health, were worried the malaise might be some form of contagion that could affect them.

Notwithstanding this I immediately went to his place of retreat to hammer upon the door demanding that I may be admitted and on convincing him that I was indeed alone he unlocked it and bade me enter.

My friend had been a hale and hearty man when I last saw him but what stood before me was a mere shadow of his former self, his emaciated frame was wrapped in an old robe that I remembered from our college days and his cheeks were sunken in but that was not what shocked me most. His skin flesh and bone had become translucent and worse still he was lit from within with a blue glow enabling me to see into and through his very skull, Victor then threw off the robe to reveal his skeleton and internal organs which though translucent were clearly visible through the skin as though he were an anatomical model made of pale blue glass. Horrified, I asked what I could do to help but he calmly assured me that he had never felt so well in his life and he was merely holding on as long as possible that I may witness the final stage of his remarkable transition to another form. I beseeched him to return with me to St Aidan's where our medical research faculty could perhaps help him but he merely smiled again and bid me observe as before my eyes he became ever more transparent, finally fading to a mere outline. His last whispered words to me were that he would now live forever on the astral plane and with that he disappeared before my eyes. I gave Soames the briefest of explanations and then to my great shame flew back to Oxford, returning on the soonest train and once at the college went straight to my quarters to collapse in shock, causing Evelyn much concern at finding me in such a state when she visited later.

Before leaving Victor's home I had taken the crystal and the next day had the metal box in which it resided sealed in a lead container before burying it deep in the ground. Its whereabouts shall go to the grave with me and I hope it is never found.

A. Guthridge (Professor of Arcane Studies, St Aidan's)

Chapter Five – The séance

"Is there anybody there?" asked the clairvoyant in a voice as flamboyant and dramatic as her manner of dress.

Twelve others sat around the table with hands joined while holding their breath as a cold breeze blew through the dimly lit room to swirl the smoke from the incense burners.

"Is there anybody there?" her voice rang out once again and a distant trumpet-like wail was heard as if in answer.

A man in eastern garb and wearing a natty fez stood and picked up a gong to run the striker around its edge to make a continual ringing as the woman began a low moaning. One of the sitters, a studious man in tweed, suppressed a snigger only for the fez wearer to glare angrily at him.

"Is there anybody there?" repeated Madame Hecate, a ghost-like figure appeared briefly behind her and with widened eyes she threw back her turbaned head. After letting out a loud sigh the medium appeared to enter a trancelike state.

A drum sounded briefly as the assistant moved to her side to demand. "Who are you, spirit?"

"It is I, Chief Running Deer, what is it you desire of me?" her voice had changed, deepening in timbre and affecting a strange accent.

People around the table asked questions in turn, most of which regarded deceased relatives and the majority of the sitters appeared happy with her answers until a pretty young blonde nervously spoke. "I'd like to ask the *Chief* a question."

"Quickly madam, before the spirit leaves her!" urged the robed man.

"I would like to contact my poor dear mother!" requested the belle in her cut-glass accent.

"I will attempt to locate her, what is your name child?" asked the medium with a gruff deep voice.

"Elizabeth Montague, my mother's name was also Elizabeth," she replied.

The medium began her low moaning again until finally *Running Deer* answered. "Child, she is here, would you like to speak to her?" The young woman nodded and the medium's voice changed once more to that of an old woman. "Lizzy, is that you?"

"Yes mother, but I am baffled for you always called me Beth before you passed over?"

"It is quite easy to forget the trappings of mortal existence in the afterlife Beth."

"Then you are at rest now, mother?" asked Elizabeth.

"I am dear, my suffering is over." replied *mother*.

"That is curious, the doctor told me your passing was swift and without suffering my dear mother?" queried the young woman.

"No death can be without some distress, Beth, my time here is limited I fear I must go now!" replied *mother* quickly.

The man in tweed stood, breaking the circle of joined hands. "This charade, this pretence of a séance has gone on long enough!"

"Do not break contact it is very dangerous!" shouted *fez*.

"Piffle!" retorted the studious man to the shock of the other sitters.

"Piffle?" interjected the clairvoyant in annoyance, sitting forward and now quite free of her trance.

"You madam are nothing more than a money grabbing charlatan, taking advantage of grieving people who are desperate for word from their loved ones!" he continued.

"How dare you make such an accusation, it is an insult to me and these poor bereaved souls?" she inquired.

"It is a good show, I'll grant you that. Your vocal skill is quite remarkable but your ghostly noises are nothing more than bellows and horns and your ethereal spirit merely a *Pepper's Ghost* projected from behind the false mirror yonder, you madam, are no more in touch with the spirit world than I." insisted the man in tweed.

"How dare you insult Madame Hecate, she is the greatest medium alive?" snarled the fez-wearer angrily.

"So great that she could not detect my plant among the sitters?" countered the man. "How is your mother, by the way, Claire?"

"Mama is alive and very well, thank you Professor," replied *Elizabeth* in a voice more Parisian than polite society.

"If Madame Wotsit here was anything of a seer she would have noticed the old gentleman lingering by Mrs. Raleigh." exclaimed a weasel-like fellow in a brown suit and bowler hat, he was pointing to an elderly woman.

"And who may I ask are you?" demanded Madame Hecate furiously.

"This is Mr. Sidney Parret, an acquaintance of mine who, unlike you, is a genuine clairvoyant," explained the Professor.

"Fake, if ever I saw one!" declared the weasel assuredly, his arms crossed.

Then gesturing to another the Professor continued. "And this fellow here is Mr. Cooper, a reporter from the Daily Herald.

As the other sitters clustered around the fraudulent pair to demand their money back a giant of a man threw open the door to advance menacingly towards the Professor and his companions only to pull up sharply as the diminutive Parisian pulled a stiletto and gestured threateningly towards him.

"Good night Mrs. Hickey, for that is your true name I believe?" said the Professor at the door. "You can look forward to reading all about your fraudulent practise in the Herald tomorrow."

Before the quartet left Parret quickly took the elbow of Mrs. Raleigh to say. "Your Herbert says the cashbox is hidden in an alcove behind the bookcase in his study and you're not to let his brother Cecil anywhere near it!" he winked at her before joining his companions to leave the angry hubbub behind.

CHAPTER SIX – THE SHAPE

Aaron Bergman was a little the worse for drink, he had met with his friend Rudolph earlier for a quick gin, one drink had led to another and at midnight he staggered from the Seven Bells. His friend had left much earlier to catch the omnibus and return to his premises to ensure the ovens were warming, he had been complaining about his lazy apprentice on and off for most of the night.

Although most of the former members of the *Hand* lived within a short distance of each other, Aaron and Rudi were the only ones who kept in regular contact. Since coming to London nine years ago the former *fingers* had made new lives for themselves, Bergman, now a boatman, was currently employed at Brentford dock where he eased his social conscience by fighting to secure better pay and conditions for his fellow workers and was considered something of a firebrand. Rudi Meisel owned a successful bakery in Golders Green and had married a local girl with whom he fathered two children, Samuel, the religious one, was now a rabbi who always had a warm greeting when approached but otherwise kept his old colleagues at a distance. Ticho, the last of the fingers, had taken up his former trade as a goldsmith and barely acknowledged their existence, *but then Franz had always been a miserable bastard!*

None of them liked to discuss the old days much.

As he meandered back to his boat Aaron took a scrap of parchment from his pocket and examined it in the wan light of a street lamp, it was written in a very old script and he could make no sense of it, *perhaps Samuel could translate it for him?* A sudden noise made him start and turning, the man saw a shape looming out the darkness to come straight for him accompanied by heavy clumping footfalls.

Bergman did not tarry to see who it was but ran towards the dock, *it was no doubt some thug hired by old man Millward!* His policy of standing up for the rights of the working man often incurred the wrath of a boss and this was not the first time he had been ambushed on his way home. He planned to lose his pursuer in the maze of rickety old buildings along the waterfront and if he could get behind them all the better, one good blow from the *leveller*, a sturdy stick he always carried, would quickly sort things out.

Having gained on his would-be assailant Bergman took cover in the gap between two sheds to catch his breath, there came the curious clumping again and the shape appeared before him silhouetted against the glow from the dock lights.

Gasping in astonishment the man swung his cudgel high only for it to bounce off the figure's head with a clack! It thrust out a shovel-sized hand to grab his head pulling him from his hiding place to squeeze Bergman's skull hard, upon hearing it crack the hand threw his limp corpse from the quayside to fall in the river like a discarded rag doll.

Chapter Seven – The Brass Telescope and the Woe it Brought

Guthridge finished writing up the exposé of Madame Hecate using notes scribbled in the dim light of the railway carriage on his return journey to Oxford then turned back a few pages of his journal and there it was.

Friday, June 14th 1901.

I received word that Professor Ulysses Bumstead, a renowned scholar from the University of Boston, was in London to give a presentation on metaphysics and my interest was piqued. My opinion of the man, who in all truth ran a small office in the bowels of the aforesaid institution, was that he was little more than a charlatan heralding from the deep-south, often exaggerating the results of his research into the arcane. Nonetheless, I purchased tickets for Paddington Station and accompanied by my dearest Evelyn, set off for the capital.

Bumstead's talk was in itself nothing I had not heard

before and the man did little more, in my humble opinion, than put a new interpretation on the writings of Aristotle and the works of the German polymath Leibnitz (*a contemporary of Newton's I might add!*). We of course, had the usual problem in entering the Debating Society's chambers in that they were going to bar entry to Evelyn simply because she was a woman (*this belief that the opposite sex is somehow intellectually inferior often causes me to become infuriated!*) and I was in the process of politely stating that the gentler sex were making great strides in the scientific community when the redoubtable Miss Poole, taking up the gauntlet, began arguing forcibly with the ushers. Bumstead himself appeared on hearing the ruckus outside and insisted that *a lady as lovely as her* be allowed to attend, Evelyn was quite taken with the man's gracious manner and I admit to being a little jealous at this for he was closer to her in age than I and possessed the sort of dashing good looks women seem to favour.

Following his discourse the American sought out the pair of us and to my surprise informed me that he had fervently hoped I would attend today informing me that he possessed an object, a family heirloom which used correctly might unlock a doorway to another dimension. I scoffed at this but he insisted we return to his hotel to examine it. I somewhat reluctantly agreed but Evelyn, impressed by the man's suave manner, was more than eager to see his artefact.

Once at the Berkeley Hotel, Bumstead proudly showed off his treasure, it resembled nothing so much as a large brass telescope of non-euclidian cross-section with a multi-faceted crystal lens at each end. The outer surface of the cylinder was completely smooth but the rim that mounted each of the crystals was engraved all around with symbols that had a disturbingly familiar appearance. Bumstead asked me, in his drawling accent, what I made of his treasure and after examining it noticed scratches on the polished surface. I suggested it would fit into or through something and he excitedly agreed informing me that I was correct in this assumption but that the location of the device was important for its operation, I asked where that was and he replied somewhere in England, the answer, he claimed could be found by translating his great-uncle's notebook (*which of course he had brought with him*) written in a curious mixture of Latin, Aramaic and impressions of a strange cuneiform script. I replied that I would consider it and since we had nothing planned for the next few days we took a room in the same hostelry. My recent experience with my unfortunate friend Victor had dampened my enthusiasm for arcane adventure and I felt uncertain about giving my assistance to this undertaking, particularly since the crystal lenses had the same blue hue as the infernal gem that had affected my old acquaintance so greatly. Evelyn, on the other hand was quite taken with the idea and being something of an expert in archaic languages offered to help translate the script with Bumstead. I was uneasy at the thought of her being alone with the handsome American but, as she reminded me later that night she was her own woman and I had no control over her. Evie has the talent to make me most amenable to her suggestions and later I somewhat reluctantly agreed not to stand in the way.

We returned to Oxford the very next day with Bumstead in tow, installing him in my quarters while I moved in with Evie for the duration of his stay, this quite outlandish arrangement was suggested by my beloved herself (*in an attempt, I believe, to quash any worries I had of her fidelity*).

For a few weeks things went well, I returned to my lectures while Evelyn enthusiastically assisted Bumstead in his translation, often returning home exhilarated and talking excitedly of the advances they had made with the strange script and how she desired to visit America one day. I won't go into detail but she seemed quite invigorated by this activity and became very attentive to my needs.

For my part I remembered where I had seen the symbols engraved on the lens mounts, they were a rare type of cuneiform I had seen only within the pages of the Key of Muati, an ancient tome kept locked away in the Bodleian Library and accessible exclusively to permitted scholars. Muati was a rather obscure Sumerian deity associated with a mysterious island paradise called Dilmun, I warned "Lee" as Evie was wont to call him, of the dangers of Sumerian mysticism but it was to no avail. Finally, when enough of his great uncle's notebook was deciphered Bumstead took us to the most expensive restaurant in Oxford to celebrate his (and Evie's) success.

Over dinner he recounted that a fossilised tree stump in Windsor Forest known as the Devil's Oak was possessed of a familiar shaped hole through its trunk and planned a sortie there that weekend. He oozed southern charm throughout the evening and I could not but help but notice Evie's rapt attention or how she hung on his every word so I sought solace in the rather fine brandy the establishment served.

I cannot recall how I got to my bed that night but awoke next morning with a splitting headache. Evelyn could not look me in the eye during breakfast and I had the vaguest memory of waking briefly from my drunken stupor to find her not at my side. With a heavy heart I decided it would be for the best not to press the point.

Our relationship became strained over the next few days until we finally journeyed to Windsor on the Friday to join Bumstead, who was already there. Upon our arrival he grinned widely, Evie hardly spoke a word to him in greeting but he seemed to neither notice nor care.

Our party hired a horse and carriage to drive to the wood and on the way Bumstead boasted that in America motorcars were becoming commonplace as a mode of transport. I countered that in Great Britain the internal combustion engine would never supplant the horse but Evie snapped at this, saying I needed to move more with the times and I crossly reminded her that as an exceptional horsewoman herself she ought to be more supportive. Up-on hearing this Bumstead made a remark asking if she rode side-saddle or astride the horse as women often did in the USA, with a flushed face she admitted to the latter, at which he grinned saying he was not at all surprised at her preference to be astride. I have to say that whatever had occurred between Evie and the American he was no gentleman and seemed to relish her discomfort, sadly I *am* a gentleman and found myself loathe to call him out without good cause (*besides I am no pugilist and he was much younger and fitter than I*).

Finally, we arrived at our somewhat disappointing destination, set upon a slight knoll it was most certainly a fossilised tree stump but scarcely more than five feet tall with the hole a little more than twelve inches above the ground. I held my humour in check as we lay down to peer through at each other and when my beloved peeped at me she smiled for the first time that day, raising my spirits somewhat. Bumstead then extended the telescopic device and inserted it slowly into the orifice while winking and casting a wry smile at Evie, who looked away.

We waited for a while but nothing happened, the American looked perplexed and I to my shame, sniggered at his failure. He became angry and berated me for my lack of consideration which made me laugh all the more, then sneeringly, *Lee* told me of the less than scholarly activities he and Evie had embarked upon when supposedly deciphering the Sumerian code.

Shocked, I asked her if it were true and she tearfully confessed, informing me that on the night of my drunk she had, after getting me home, spent the major part of it in his bed where he asked her to come with him to Boston upon his return to America. She had demurred and Bumstead demanded that she choose between him and the *crusty old professor* come the weekend.

Anger, the like of which I had never known before, rose up in me and I threw myself upon the scoundrel. The

American being younger and fitter quickly got in several blows while Evie, pulling ineffectually at his arm, screamed for the carriage driver to assist as we wrestled like the fools we were. The stout fellow dragged the American away and my beloved helped me up while crying that this was all because of her folly.

Bumstead meanwhile tussled with the carriage-man and after knocking him to the ground, advanced on us in a state of rage. Not one of us was watching the tree where a shaft of sunlight falling upon the narrow end of the *telescope* caused the petrified oak to pulsate with an eldritch blue glow and begin generating an eerie droning.

All three of us turned at the strange sound and in astonishment saw a phenomenon, a tendril of the same blue hue as the crystal snaked out from the wider lens and Bumstead, standing directly in its path, was grabbed by the ankle to be pulled to the floor.

The azure tentacle began dragging him towards the glowing bole from whence it originated, struggling against he shouted for help and in spite of the disdain I felt for the man I threw myself on the floor to grab his hands, only for it to relentlessly draw me along with him. The carriage-man having come to his senses, rushed to my assistance and grabbing a hand each we dug in our heels to begin an insane tug of war with the tendril as our opponent and Bumstead as the rope. In spite of our best efforts, our sinews straining and his cries echoing in our ears, the eldritch terror was winning, pulling him ever closer to the crystal. His feet touched it and the blue glow fanned out spreading along his legs which began to narrow and you can imagine our horror as he began to be funnelled into it. When his legs had been swallowed to the knee I felt something pop as his arm dislocated and I let go in alarm, his screams doubled then stopped suddenly and the ashen-faced driver realising his effort was to no avail did likewise. The three of us just stood there helplessly watching the late Ulysses Bumstead (*as he now most certainly was*) being steadily squeezed and siphoned into a petrified tree. When he had gone the blue light cut off sharply and an eerie silence fell only to be broken by six loud reports as Evie sobbing bitterly, discharged all the chambers of her Webley into the *telescope* to render it useless forever. Whatever purpose this awful device served and why it needed the petrified oak to operate we would now never know.

When all was done and over with we sat in my beloved's parlour in Oxford where I raised the courage to ask Evie what choice she would have made.

She looked at me with tears in her eyes and replied simply. "The right one!"

A. Guthridge (Professor of Arcane Studies, St Aidan's)

He closed the journal and regarded her photograph with sadness in his heart, *had it been only six weeks ago?* He wasn't that sorry the man had perished but the awful manner of his passing still haunted him and every day without Evie was a torment, *why did I treat her so dreadfully?*

Chapter Eight – The Truth of the Parchment

Franz Ticho exited the synagogue shaking his head in disbelief, *it was complete and utter nonsense, of course,* Samuel was a very learned man but Ticho believed he was letting his imagination get the better of him this time. Early this morning, he had found a scrap of parchment pushed under the front door and finding he was unable to read the archaic writing had taken it to the evening service where following the Amidah he had shown it to the rabbi, an old acquaintance.

The holy man had paled in fright on seeing it before producing an identical list. "I received this yesterday, it is a list of names, all our names!" his friend had explained.

"So are you so scared of a list, I wonder many how many times my name was written on a list by an enemy and yet here I am still?" he had boasted.

"But Franz, this is from *him*, don't you understand that?" the holy man had asked, clearly uneasy.

Ticho had cast his eyes over the parchment to say. "I see four lines in a script I can't read and another on the back, other than you I doubt if any of the Hand could translate this and I include him in that!" he had retorted.

The rabbi then anxiously pointed at each name in turn. "Here is Aaron then you, next is Rudolph and finally me, the word on the other side translates as truth. It's him I tell you, he has found us and he wants revenge!"

"Even if that's true, what can he do to us?" asked Ticho. "All those years in Pankrác will have left him a broken man."

"You have no idea of the significance of this, Franz." the rabbi had replied nervously.

"Then tell me, Samuel, why does a piece of parchment cause you such great concern?" Ticho had asked and his friend explained its significance at great length while railing about the terrible thing he feared had been unleashed by the man they had betrayed.

Once out on the street, Ticho had found himself looking nervously over his shoulder, had the old man's mood rubbed off on him? *Nothing more than that,* he told himself quickening his step nonetheless. He waved to the baker stacking fresh bagels in a nearby shop window getting ready for the evening rush when shift workers would flock to buy them on their way home, *another name on the list according to the rabbi!*

It seemed very dark as he approached his premises, were the gaslights dimmer than usual or was it just his imagination? There came a noise from the gloom of a nearby alley, a sound like the scraping of stone upon stone and by peering hard Ticho could make out the shape of a tall figure lurking in the shadows.

"Who are you?" demanded Ticho but there was no answer, the figure just stood immobile in the dark.

Ticho shook his head and was unlocking the door to his property when the noise sounded again and looking back into the street saw what it was charging towards him faster than anything of that bulk had a right to. *Damn it, Samuel had been right after all!* He ducked as it swung a massive fist to miss him while smashing the door into splinters but as he made for the stairs to his workshop a second blow caught his leg causing him to yell in pain as something broke. His assailant was now having difficulty negotiating the narrow stairwell, its wide shoulders scoring gouges in the plaster on the walls as it forced its way slowly up giving Ticho enough time to crawl painfully to the top and into his workshop. Once inside he managed to push the heavy door shut and after throwing the bolts turned the lock, a goldsmith by trade his workroom was very secure. Ticho began crawling painfully across the wooden floor on hands and knees with the intention of reaching the desk where he kept his pistol. *Let's see how you stand up to a bullet!* But before he could reach it and to his great dismay the sturdy oak door flew open and the monstrosity forced its way through the broken frame to enter the room and stomp to where he lay, shaking the very floor as it drew near.

The terrified goldsmith raised his head to see the horror standing there patiently as if waiting for instruction, the Hebrew word for truth was written on its forehead and the eyes glittered like glass marbles. "May God forgive me, we only did what we had to!" he cried as it raised a foot to stomp once more.

Chapter Nine – Visitors

Guthridge had finished his lectures for the morning so after picking up his mail from the porter's lodge, he sat down to read the Oxford Gazette. There was an article about him with the lurid title, *University Professor's crusade against fraudulent Clairvoyants* in which it mentioned Madame Hecate and several other supposed mediums he had exposed over the past few weeks. His concentration was broken by a rapping at the door and opening it saw a familiar figure stood there.

"Good day Inspector Poulson do come in, to what do I owe this pleasure?"

"And a good day to you Arnold" the policeman seemed perturbed. "I'll come straight to the point, we've a strange murder on our hands and with you being an expert in all things odd I thought I'd consult you, strictly off the record of course" Guthridge had helped Scotland Yard several times in the past.

"Of course Daniel, anything to help His Majesty's Constabulary." *and it will perhaps take my mind off Evelyn.*

Poulson opened his briefcase to place a photograph on the Professor's desk. "A man was murdered in Golders Green last night and I'll warn you now, Arnold, it is not a pretty sight."

"Good Lord! Was his head put under a steam press?" exclaimed Guthridge in shock. The picture showed a man, judging by his attire, spread-eagled upon the floor head crushed flat, blood and brain matter was splattered around the remains of the cranium. Guthridge sat heavily in his leather chair. "I feel a little queasy, Daniel, could you get me a brandy and by all means have one yourself."

The Inspector poured two good measures from the decanter on Guthridge's desk and handed the Professor a glass. "I shouldn't really drink on duty Arnold, but bugger it!" he took a sip. "Oh that's good, you always have the best grog, mind if I sit down?" Guthridge motioned to a chair and the policeman gladly took a seat. "That photo doesn't show the half of it, not a nice death by any means and in answer to your question, no, a steam press wasn't involved. The deceased was a goldsmith named Franz Ticho and it appears he was killed in his workshop by something stamping on his head with enough force to do that!"

"An elephant perhaps, is there a circus nearby?" asked the Professor.

"No and how would you get one up the stairs?" he rolled his eyes. "I did do a check with the Zoo regardless and none of theirs are missing. Now, this is where you come in, we found dried clay all over the place including a large concentration on what was left of his skull, the floor, the doors and in scrape-marks along the walls of the staircase. To top it off there were several reports of a giant shape or figure moving through the shadows a couple of streets away last night.

"Have you tried fingerprinting for clues, I hear it's becoming quite widespread in many forces? They caught a murderer in Argentina using the process several years ago."

"Arnold, Scotland Yard is not manned by Neanderthals you know? There seemed little point in fingerprinting anything as the place was in such a bloody mess and I mean that quite literally!" retorted the policeman.

"Daniel, I'm at a loss to see how I can help" remarked Guthridge.

"Oh, come on Arnold, this death has got what's that word you use, paranormal, written all over it?" stated Poulson. "The door at street level had been smashed to pieces and the oak door at the top of the stairs had been pushed open with such force that not only had it broken the lock but two sturdy bolts *and* twisted its hinges into the bargain, all of them made of steel! Look, I'll leave you a copy of the case notes, please have a look while I continue the investigation back in London. What do you say, Arnold?"

Guthridge half-reluctantly agreed and when the policeman had left for his train began to look through the notes, carefully turning the grisly photograph over so he would not see it again until quite ready. Poulson had not been gone five minutes where there was a knock at his door once again and thinking the inspector had forgotten something he opened it to see Evelyn's niece standing there.

"Good afternoon Lady Mary, it's a pleasure to see you and something of a surprise. You are well I trust?"

"Good afternoon to you Arnold and I am very well, thank you," Guthridge showed her inside. Mary sat in the chair so recently vacated by Poulson and glancing curiously at the empty brandy bowls opined. "A bit early in the day, isn't it?"

"Had a bit of a shock," he explained. "Can I get you anything?"

"A cup of tea would be nice, thank you." Guthridge put the kettle on and nervously set out the crockery, *what did she want?* Leaving it to boil he re-joined Mary in the study, noticing how much she resembled Evie apart from having lighter hair but there was something different about the young woman he could not put his finger on. "Professor, don't linger by the kitchen door, please sit" she insisted as if talking to a servant while removing her fine gloves.

"What can I do for you, Lady Mary?"

"Answer me this one question, why haven't you visited my aunt since her return to Oxford?" she replied sharply.

"I was away in London until yesterday and come to that, I was not aware that Evelyn had returned?"

"I see, well I'm telling you now!"

"I doubt she would be very eager to see me again?" remarked Guthridge despondently.

"Hah! You don't know that."

"Mary, I was rather beastly to her and we did not part on good terms."

"I know" she informed Guthridge tersely.

"Evelyn told you?" he asked in horror.

"Auntie sent a telegram to me almost begging me to let her stay with us and upon arriving she seemed rather distraught and locked herself in her bedroom to cry for a whole day. Arnold, you must understand that Aunt Evelyn has always been a pillar of strength to me and to see her like that caused me such great concern that I prevailed upon her to tell me why she was in such a state."

"Oh dear lord, so you know what a brute I was to her?"

"She related the whole sorry business to me, Arnold, I could not believe that you were capable of such a thing and said as such. Auntie then revealed all that had happened between her and that awful Bumstead fellow, I believe your behaviour to have been an aberration brought on by the anxiety that you might have lost her to him and told her so."

"What did she say to that?"

"Why not find out for yourself?"

"But Mary I dare not, she would not want to see me."

"But I insist that you do!" he found himself drawn into her very blue eyes. "Do as I request Arnold Guthridge, it is not too much to ask is it?"

The academic could feel his will weakening *it wouldn't hurt to visit her surely?* The kettle on the kitchen hob began to boil, its whistling breaking him from his reverie. "I knew you had changed since our last meeting Mary, when did you acquire the power of mesmerism?"

"That is a story for another day Professor. I shall ask you once again with no further attempt at coercion, will you please visit my Aunt Evelyn?"

Chapter Ten – Calling on Evie

Guthridge's heart leapt upon seeing Evelyn as she answered the door with her dark-blonde hair down and wearing the silk robe he so much admired her in. "Hello Arnold, you look well." her voice was strained, her expression unreadable.

"Evie, I didn't realise you were back in Oxford until the other day, it's so good to see you again." he blurted out, a lump in his throat.

She bade him enter and he sat in one of her comfortable chintz chairs while she took the seat opposite. "I returned to Oxford but a few days ago Arnold."

"Yes, so I understand, you are well, Evie?" the strain between them was palpable.

"I am, thank you, I understand that my niece came to see you?"

"Yes, that girl has changed, there is something different about her." asserted Guthridge.

"You have no idea!" exclaimed Evelyn then asked curiously. "Did she try to mesmerise you by any chance?"

"Yes, she did!"

"I expressly forbade her to do that!" she replied crossly before changing the subject. "I hear you have been unmasking fraudulent clairvoyants?"

"Indeed, I have a useful ally in genuine sensitive called Sidney Parret and there is a young actress in my employ who infiltrates séances at my behest. Sidney and I will then pounce when the fraud fails to spot her, usually with an eager reporter to record proceedings."

"It is good that you are keeping busy when not lecturing," she remarked politely.

Guthridge looked into her very blue eyes and could hold himself back no longer. "Evie, can you ever forgive me for how I behaved?"

She considered her response before asking. "I have just one question Arnold, why?"

"I have no excuse other than that I was consumed with a jealous desire to take back what I felt had been stolen." Guthridge was contrite.

"You do not own me!" she cried in vexation. "You forced yourself upon me for that?"

Guthridge had brooded upon Evie's enigmatic answer following the business with Bumstead until finally his normally even-tempered composure had snapped and tearing Evelyn's clothes he had taken her most savagely, she did not struggle but merely lay submissively with tears in her eyes. When the act was over, Arnold, appalled at what he had done fell upon his knees before her to apologise profusely and Evelyn had calmly told him to leave. She had departed to stay at Pendleberry Hall shortly afterwards and he had not seen her since.

"Evie, I behaved like a brute, I wish it were possible to undo what was done."

"I never refused your advances in all our time together even when Lee and I were... I, I appreciate you were hurt and upset about my frisson with him, but what you did made me feel worthless!"

"I believed you had intended to leave me for that puffed-up popinjay, Evelyn, I have no excuse for my behaviour. I behaved like a cad, little better than a common ruffian."

"Oh my dear, Lee swept me off my feet and he was so…" her voice tailed off, she was about to say virile, remembering passionate encounters over the large oak desk in Guthridge's study but decided it was a bad idea. "It was exhilarating, it was exciting and I felt like a silly young girl caught up in a whirlwind completely, if mistakenly, smitten with him."

"You said you would have made the right choice?"

"I had become extremely fond of Lee despite everything and *was* in truth considering going with him to America but his improper behaviour that day and the way he taunted you made me see him in his true light. I was very upset upon our return to Oxford for I had just watched this man, this man who I had feelings for, being pulled and squeezed into that infernal device and wasn't thinking clearly. In hindsight he was a vain braggart satisfying his ego by dallying with me and I was ridden with guilt, thinking you were by far the better person, but what you did shocked me and I am not easily shocked as you well know."

"So what would have been your choice?" asked Guthridge.

"I would have chosen you, you idiot!" she snapped.

"Evie, what happened between you and the American, you have my word I shall never hold it against you."

"Thank you Arnold, that is perhaps more than I deserve."

"Please say you forgive me Evie for I love you with all my heart." declared Guthridge.

"You have my forgiveness Arnold, for when all is said and done neither of us is without shame and I have known for a long time that you love me, I just wish I could say the same in reply" she said in a tremulous voice.

"Then it is over?" Guthridge, heartbroken stood up to leave. "Have I lost you forever because of my stupidity?"

anything!" he laughed again. "The weird thing is it's as if his head was grabbed by a large hand and subjected to enough pressure to crush the skull like an eggshell. Have you heard from your *expert* yet?"

"No, he's still sulking in Oxford" replied Poulson.

"Have you tried the British Museum?"

"Yes, they say it's an ancient form of Hebrew or some such, the only word they could read was *truth*, the buggers wanted to keep hold of it."

"Hebrew, it's something to do with the Jews then, eh?"

Before he could answer a police constable entered the morgue to pass Poulson a telegram. "Well blow me down, our expert is coming in on the next train and wants me to meet him at the station," he announced after reading it.

***

"Well Sidney what can you feel?" asked Guthridge, he had Poulson pick up the medium from his lodgings on the way from Paddington Station. Parret was already waiting for them when they arrived gleefully claiming the spirits had informed him of their imminent arrival, the professor thought it more likely the excellent view of the street afforded by the upstairs window of his room had more to do with it. Still, there was no doubting the little man had true psychic ability.

Parret was staring at the dried stain where only a few days earlier Ticho's squashed brains had decorated the floor. "He was scared stiff, something 'orrid was after him!" his eyes widened. "Oh lawks, he was scared, pain, his leg, the right one, he was on his belly crawling, trying to reach his gun" Sidney's breathing became rapid. "Let's see how you stand up to a bullet!" the medium shouted, then screamed and staggered back as Poulson moved a chair to catch him.

He sat down heavily as Guthridge held out a hip flask

containing his excellent brandy. "What was it, did you see anything Sidney?"

"The "truth" that was the last thing he saw, that and those eyes, glittering like glass alleys."

"He saw the truth? Then you know who did it?" asked the inspector, the young constable with them looked as white as a sheet.

"Nah, it was the word "Truth" in that funny scribble like you see round 'ere and it weren't no man what did this, it was something huge with 'orrible eyes!" he replied, raising the brandy to his lips.

"Huge enough to scrape its shoulders on the narrow stairwell?" ventured Guthridge.

The man took another swig from the flask. "Yeah, big and wide it was, I can't get no more from 'ere Prof', sorry."

"Was there a gun?" Guthridge asked the police inspector.

"Yes in that desk and the chap's leg was broken. How did he know that?"

"Sidney is one of those rare things, Daniel, a genuine clairvoyant, no tricks, no stage magic, just a mind in touch with the ethereal plane."

"You're hiding summat, Inspector!" said Parret suddenly. "It's the truth!"

Shaking his head in disbelief, Poulson gestured to the constable who passed him a folder and opening it revealed a scrap of parchment with unintelligible characters on it. "You're a clever fellow, Mr. Parret. We found this in one of the deceased's pockets."

He handed it to Guthridge who examined it then turning it over remarked. "I can't read the other side but this word says "truth" in Hebrew!"

"Yes, that's all the museum could work out, I knew you would be the right person to ask Arnold" stated Poulson.

"Daniel, could I take this back to Oxford? I know a certain lady there who is something of an expert in ancient languages" he had immediately thought of Evie.

"Yes by all means, Arnold, you know a lady who's an expert in languages you say? Good lord, whatever next?"

Parret gave a knowing smile. "Ask him why there's two of 'em?"

"Damn me, we could do with you at Scotland Yard!" exclaimed Poulson. "You're bloody right, of course" and turning another page exposed a second parchment. "Near enough identical and found on the body of a man we fished out of the Brent this morning. His head was crushed, not as much as this chap's" he nodded towards the stain. "But certainly bad enough to kill him instantly, it was almost as if a giant hand had squeezed it to leave finger-marks in his cranium."

"These murders must be connected!" exclaimed the professor.

"It is the work of a single individual or group, of that I am certain." asserted Poulson.

"Bloody 'ell!" remarked Parret before attacking Guthridge's brandy again.

"Did you find any clay on the body?" asked the professor.

"Arnold, old chap, he'd been in the water for at least a day possibly more, I'm rather afraid anything like that would have been washed off during his immersion, not only that the fish and god alone knows what else had eaten his eyes and nose, his face is a right mess and we still don't know who he is."

The medium started in alarm. "Gawd help us, I ain't going nowhere near that one!"

"Fair enough Sidney, you have been of invaluable assistance, you may go" stated Inspector Poulson and deftly retrieving Guthridge's hip flask handed it back to him as Parret left. "Incredible!" stated the inspector.

"Yes, a very talented individual. Daniel, we are in Golders Green, have you shown this parchment to any of the rabbi's around here?"

"Arnold, I know I'm little more than a flatfooted bobby but give me some credit."

"And?" asked Guthridge unrepentant.

"There are three synagogues in the area, all of the rabbis could read the word "truth" on the back, one suggested the remainder was Kabbalistic but written in an ancient form of Hebrew, another got very upset and ordered me out of his synagogue, the last a man called Goldman went pale and chanted something under his breath before saying he could recognise evil when he saw it and of course, claimed he couldn't translate it."

"Or wouldn't, perhaps?" ventured Guthridge.

"Yes, they're quite reluctant to let us gentiles in on their strange ways."

"Hardly a surprise when you consider how we *gentiles* have treated them over the ages?" opined the professor.

Chapter Twelve – The Conspirators

Rabbi Schul removed the Shem from the slot like mouth then climbed down the short stepladder to set the parchment alight over a candle.

"Why do you always burn the Shem?" asked Koen bringing over a bucket of wet clay.

"So that it may not be used again" replied the old man peering over his half-moon glasses.

"I thought the script was written for a specific target?" he asked, climbing the steps Schul had just vacated.

"If the name was erased and the Shem replaced, our creation would reanimate without true purpose and that could be a very bad thing indeed, it would be difficult to control and could attack upon a whim!"

"When will you teach me to write the Shem, Isaac?" Koen smoothed down the fresh clay he had put into the wide cracks on its arms and shoulders.

"It took a lot of damage pursuing Ticho, better to let the clay rest for a day" replied the old man while watching Koen work.

"And the Shem?" inquired the other.

"It will need a good soaking to help it bind" continued Schul.

"You haven't answered my question, Rabbi!" snapped Koen.

"Oy, it is Isaac when you want something and Rabbi otherwise, don't think I haven't noticed, Joseph."

"I'm sorry my old friend, but I am impatient to end this. What if anything happened to you?" asked Koen in a more conciliatory tone.

"But if I were to show you, you would no longer need me."

"Do you not trust me?"

"You are too eager for revenge and it is a dish best served cold so I hear?"

"I spent nine years in that cesspit because of their betrayal!" protested Koen angrily.

"And I was there two years earlier because of Adler or whatever he calls himself now and that's why I want him to be last, jumping at his own shadow" replied Schul calmly.

"I envy you your patience, Isaac."

"We will begin your tuition tomorrow but we must let our creation rest for a few days, this will also lull Adler into a false sense of security."

"Thank you Isaac, I apologise for my outburst." Koen stood back to admire his handiwork. "There, good as new."

"Hardly that I think, but it will do for now. So how is the other one coming along?"

"It is going well, it will not long before it's ready I think?" Joseph ascended the steps once again to pour a pail of water over its head and shoulders.

"I'm still not happy about hiring goys to do this."

"They are fine craftsmen and they worked on some of London's grandest projects last century."

"But they are not of the faith"

"Why does it matter, they are less likely to know what they are creating because of that and anyway they will not live to spread the word afterwards."

"You will kill them?" asked the Rabbi, *revenge was one thing, but killing innocent people?*

"Yes we must leave no trail to follow, don't worry Isaac I will handle it myself, I know you have no stomach for such a thing" replied Koen curtly.

After the Austro-Hungarians had finished torturing Joseph Koen he had been thrown him into Pankrác Prison and left to rot, he had been betrayed by his colleagues for money and a ticket out of jail but as luck would have it his cellmate was one Rabbi Isaac Schul. The man had been part of a plot against the regime two years before and had also been betrayed by one of Koen's former comrades. The cell-mates had struck up a friendship based on their shared hatred and Schul had informed him of his plan to use the teachings of the Kabbala to create a powerful weapon for use against their oppressors. The Rabbi promised to help Koen wreak his revenge, especially upon Adler who had betrayed them both and in return the younger man promised to help Schul build an army of these weapons to start a revolt in Prague, if and when they were ever released.

The chance came when the authorities, wishing to quell growing unrest in the city issued pardons for several political prisoners on the condition they leave Bohemia and never return. So it was that Koen and Schul were released and after discovering that his former colleagues had fled to England, Joseph had set off across Europe with the Rabbi in tow to seek revenge.

They had learned much from their first creation and improvements were being incorporated in the second. "We could test the new one on them?" he suggested.

"It is weapon of revenge, how could I justify using it against the innocent?" queried Schul.

"Very well I will do it, either way they'll be just as dead!" replied Koen with a shrug as he filled the bucket again, as if it was the most natural thing in the world.

"And you will teach me to write a Shem."

"Joseph, please show some patience, your time in prison should have taught you the importance of that."

Joseph Koen gave a rare smile. "Wise words old friend, one more pail I think then we'll get something to eat, I have a desire for salt beef and I know of a pub that sells a passable schnapps, one even such a holy man as you may find hard to resist."

Koen poured a final bucket over it then leaving the giant figure alone in the warehouse with light from the high windows reflecting off the glittering eyes and after locking up securely set off with Schul into the falling dusk.

Chapter Thirteen – A Reconciliation of Sorts

Lady Mary Theddingworth had opted to stay in Oxford for a while and taking a suite at the Randolph had invited her aunt to join her for afternoon tea.

"Arnold came to see me as you suggested," said Evelyn.

"And?" asked the young woman, pouring tea into two delicate china cups.

"He confessed his love of which I have known for a long time."

"And you rebuffed him didn't you?"

"How can you know that?" asked Evelyn.

"Mesmerism is not the only ability my new condition has bestowed upon me and besides, it's written all over your face."

"Mary, I do like Arnold and I am very fond of him but cannot truly say that I love him." she lied.

"Really Auntie, you say you do not love this man who you chose over the chance of immortality, I do not understand you?" snapped Mary.

"I... I thought perhaps that I loved him but he became so withdrawn following that business with his old friend, I was trying so hard to be understanding but then along came Lee, he was so dashing and so very different to Arnold" she sighed deeply, remembering the passion of their lovemaking and how well-endowed the man had been.

"Poppycock!" retorted her niece. "He was a lothario who you had known for a little over two weeks, I only met him the once and saw through the man straight away. He was just using you for his own gratification Auntie, do you seriously believe he was going to take you to America, poor Arnold, how he must have felt when he discovered how he had been cuckolded?"

"You do not know anything, child!" retorted Evelyn.

"I know that the man I that was to marry made an advance to you and was refused, the reason given was your love for another and if it wasn't the professor who was it?"

Evelyn did not answer, merely casting her gaze to the floor.

"Well?" insisted her niece.

"In spite of Arnold's dreadful behaviour I miss him, his smile, his untidiness, his gentle nature and seeing him the other day made me feel so guilty"

"So are you going to do something or do you want me to intervene again?" asked her niece.

"No, Mary, I will go and see him myself."

* * *

"Evelyn!" exclaimed Arnold in surprise. Brigg and Fenwick, two of his most promising students were there having just attended a tuition session in his study and were making ready to go.

"Hello David, so nice to see you again and you are Cornelius Brigg if I remember correctly?"

The young men exchanged courteous handshakes with her then left the Professor and Evelyn to their own devices. "Well, this is a pleasure my dear, I must confess I did not expect to see you again."

"I have spoken with Mary and she has insisted that I be honest with you."

"Oh?"

"Arnold, I was beastly to you and you treated me badly in return, the matter is closed and I dearly wish for us to be close once more."

"This is more than I could hope for, my dear," said Guthridge, holding his emotion in check.

"No physicality though, we must start again from scratch."

"I am in complete agreeance with whatever you say. Evie, does this physicality thing bar me from giving you a friendly hug?"

"No, of course not!" she smiled and they held each other for a while until Evie spotted Guthridge's large leather armchair and remembering how Lee pushed her into the soft cushions with the force of his lovemaking pulled away quickly. "That'll do for now, my love."

"Certainly my dear, I understand" he opened his desk drawer and took out a piece of parchment. "Now, believe it or not, I was considering asking for your help in deciphering this."

She scanned it quickly. "That looks like a very early form of Hebrew, there are copies of several treatises on the Talmud *and* the Kabbala in the college library that I could to use to help translate it" Evie smiled, trying not to show how overjoyed she was to be helping *her professor* with his investigations once more.

Chapter Fourteen – The Baker Turns Up The Heat

"Oh come on Samuel, are you expecting me to believe this dreck?" asked Rudi Meisel.

"Have you not heard about Franz, he is dead?" replied the Rabbi.

"Yes and I won't miss him. The man was a bastard who upset so many people that the police won't know which way to turn for suspects, everybody disliked him."

"His head was crushed, Rudi, do you not read the newspapers?"

"Yes, yes *"Horrible Murder! Goldsmith found with head stove in, police have no clue!"* it was probably a robber, after his gelt." affirmed the baker.

"No, Mrs. Spellman found him, he was making a chain for her daughter and she went to his workshop early in the morning, she said his head was flat as a blintz, brains spread all over the place. The front door was broken open and the workshop door was smashed off its hinges."

"So what, the police say it was jemmied open. The burglar probably killed him with the same crowbar?" opined Meisel uncertainly.

"Franz Ticho? The man was a brute, it would be a

foolish burglar that took him on and he kept a pistol in his workshop."

"Then there were probably more than one of them, the newspaper said his leg was broken, that would have taken the fight out of him somewhat."

"But even so?" started the Rabbi.

"It was common thieves, not some bloody monster from an old legend!"

"Have you had one of these pushed under your door?" asked Samuel holding out his parchment.

Meisel took the scrap to look closely at it. "What's this schmatta?"

"Have you seen Aaron recently?"

"A few days ago we were drinking at the Seven Bells, I left early to make sure that fool Eli had lit the ovens properly and he stayed on drinking like he does. The idiot probably got so plotzed he's still recovering on his boat!"

"Did he mention a parchment like this?"

"Oy, what is it with this parchment?"

"It's a list of names!" the Rabbi explained the parchment's significance to the disbelieving man just as he had done to Franz Ticho a day earlier.

"Aaron's sleeping off the booze on his boat, that piece of shit Ticho got murdered during a robbery, I haven't received this magical threat and you're worrying over nothing!" affirmed Bergman.

"You cannot know that!" snapped the Rabbi.

"And you do, I suppose? Our old *friend* is probably still rotting in Pankrác."

"No he isn't."

"What?"

"I recently received warning that Joseph Koen had been pardoned and exiled a year ago and worse still, a Rabbi called Isaac Schul was released with him."

"So?"

"The man is a scholar of the ancient mysteries, he could create such a thing as I have described."

"I have never heard such cockamamie drivel!" retorted Meisel. He thought for a moment then asked suspiciously. "Who would send you a message from the old country?"

"Our former captors." replied the old man honestly.

"What, do you inform on us here in London as you did Koen in Prague?"

"We all turned informer on Koen didn't we?"

Meisel didn't answer straight away then reluctantly agreed. "We had no choice if we didn't want to end up in Pankrác."

"They sent the warning as a favour for services rendered, unfortunately it took a long time to reach me."

"I can't believe you're in league with the bastard Hungarians!" snarled Meisel storming out.

The Rabbi left the synagogue a short time later and while walking home heard a news vendor shouting the latest scurrilous headlines. He stopped upon hearing the words *"body pulled from river!"* then crossed to the road to purchase a copy of the local news-sheet.

"Yesterday, workers at the Brent dock found a body floating in the river. The unfortunate man bore severe head wounds and it is thought that he may have stumbled or tripped while intoxicated and struck his head against the stonework before falling into the water. Because the man's face is unrecognisable due to the predations of fish the police are as yet unable his establish his identity, Inspector Poulson of Scotland Yard is appealing for anyone who has lost a relative or acquaintance to come forward in the hope of identifying him."

The paper went on to describe the man as middle-aged and possibly one of the itinerant workers who lived on the river a short distance from the dock works. An unnerved Samuel caught the omnibus to Brentford then walked down to the waterfront to locate Bergman's old boat. Ducking quickly under the cover he found it empty and apart from a rat gnawing at some dry bread on a plate, there was no sign of life. *This boat has been unoccupied for days, sleeping off a drunk, my arse!*

The Rabbi had confirmed his suspicion that the body recovered from the water was indeed that of Aaron Bergman.

* * *

Meisel arrived home later, sat in his chair by the fireside and picked up a copy of the local gazette to find the same news that Goldman had read. The description of the man's clothing matched what Bergman had been wearing the night they met at the Bells, there was no mention of any parchment but nonetheless it made him feel uneasy.

His youngest was playing with a wooden doll in a crib that Aaron had made for her as a gift and he spotted the girl had wrapped the doll in what looked a piece of like beige cloth.

"What is that your babe has my little dumpling?"

"It's her new blanket, I found it!" said the child triumphantly.

"Can papa see it?" he asked, the girl passed it to him and with shaking fingers he unrolled a parchment from the small wooden figure. It was almost identical to the one Adler had shown him. "Where did you find it my love?" he asked.

The child pointed to the front door. "There, on the floor, can I have Lolly back now?"

His blood ran cold. "Yes, but papa must keep her blanket" he went to the kitchen where his wife was preparing the evening meal. "Sarah, stop cooking, pack as much as you can and get the children ready, you must go to your mother's and stay there for a while!"

"But Rudi, why?" she asked, concerned at her husband's wild look.

"Please don't ask my dear, just do it, I'll help." Meisel then summoned a cab to take his family away as fast as possible. He had thought of a plan.

* * *

The bakery was sweltering hot for after sending Eli home for the night Meisel had stoked up the ovens and locked the shop door. Now all he had to do was wait, maybe it would be tonight or maybe not and he was definitely going to lose business, *but what price life?*

Meisel was dozing on a chair in the heat when it crashed through the back door. The baker had prepared for the giant's appearance and after throwing a pan of oil over the monster followed it up with a shovel of hot coals from one of the ovens to set it alight. The clay from which the thing was made began to dry and crack but even aflame it proved unstoppable and came steadily on...

* * *

Samuel Adler rushed into his home, unlocked the safe and retrieved a large tome on which was the title, *The Kabbalistic Rituals of Judah Loew ben Bezalel,* it was written in both Aramaic and ancient Hebrew and was Schul's own copy spirited away by Adler after the police had arrested the lunatic. He leafed through the pages struggling to read the archaic text before finally finding the chapter headed *Golmi* and after leaving a page holder there began the Mourner's Kaddish for Bergman. Earlier tonight he had heard the alarm bells ringing and rushing out, had followed the crowd to see Meisel's bakery ablaze and as he drew near to the conflagration he saw a face in the mass of onlookers, a face he hadn't seen in years, the man who he had given up to the authorities, the original owner of the book and his first betrayal, Rabbi Isaac Schul.

The man seemed to know he was there and turning to face him through the multitude smiled but made no attempt to pursue Adler as he fled.

Samuel, having finished the prayer, began to scrutinise the text before him. *The answer must be here somewhere!*

Chapter Fifteen – The Shem Yields its Secrets

"Arnold I've done it, the parchment is deciphered!" cried Evelyn as she burst into Guthridge's study excitedly. Four pairs of eyes turned to regard her for she had interrupted a tuition session. "Oh, please accept my apologies, I didn't realise."

"Do not apologise, Evelyn my dear," said Guthridge, the owner of one pair. "This is Mademoiselle Claire Meunier and these two gentlemen you already know" Brigg and Fenwick greeted her cordially. "Claire has come especially to Oxford to see what it is that I do."

"Bonjour, Miss Poole it is a great pleasure to meet you" said Mlle. Meunier extending her hand. "Professor Guthridge 'as told me much about you!"

"Oh, has he?" asked Evelyn, shaking the hand while regarding the pretty young woman who could only be a little older than her niece.

"Mais oui, I wanted to meet you also, the Professor he has told me how you are the cleverest, most wonderful woman he has ever known and how invaluable you are to him!" she declared in her Parisian accent.

"Oh!" Evelyn felt quite warm on hearing the complimentary words and responded in perfect French. "Merci beaucoup, madamoiselle, je suis honoré."

"Oh, bloody hell, vous parlez Francais?" exclaimed *Claire* in an accent more redolent of the East End.

"You're not French?" asked Guthridge in surprise.

"Nah Professor, I'm Sally Miller from Cheapside, born within the sound of Bow Bells." she replied.

Evelyn started laughing. "And you never suspected, Arnold?"

"Well it's not something I advertise is it? Sally Miller don't cut no mustard in the posh theatre but if you pretend to be a froggy and change your name to Claire Meunier, the nobs will queue round the block to see you" she confessed.

All were laughing now except Guthridge, embarrassed that he hadn't seen through her deception before. "Ahem, well, er, Evelyn, you have deciphered the parchment you say?"

"Yes, but…" she looked meaningfully at the trio with him.

"It's alright my dear, these two rogues you know very well and *Claire* has assisted me several times in exposing psychic fakery."

Of course, she is the actress, thought Evelyn. "Well it's a list of names and a repeated word that I am not familiar with, it's almost a litany," she opened the small notebook she carried took out a familiar parchment and laid both side by side on the leather topped desk.

The notebook had her translation, written in beautiful copperplate script.

I shall deem this list to be of They upon whom vengeance must be sought,

Aaron Bergman, traitor
The Golmi shall punish,
Franz Ticho, traitor
The Golmi shall punish,
Rudolf Meisel, traitor

The Golmi shall punish,
Rabbi Samuel Adler, the traitor of traitors
Whom the Golmi shall punish last of all

"On the reverse of the parchment is written the single word *Truth*." she informed the gathering.

Professor Guthridge scrutinised the text. "Golmi, that word rings a bell, Ticho was the man with the atrocious head injury, then there was the man found in the river with his skull crushed, I wonder if he is one of the names on your list?"

"Perhaps Inspector Poulson has made some progress in his investigation?" Evelyn bent in close to him to read her notes and he could smell her exotic, expensive perfume.

"Ahem, yes." said Guthridge gathering his wits. "I will avail myself of the phone in the porter's lodge and you students may go."

Sarah smiled as the men left. "Professor Guthridge is such a sweet man. You and him are a couple ain't you?"

"Yes, well, we're good friends. How did you come to meet him?"

"I performed in Oxford just after you went to stay with your niece, according to the Professor and he had been dragged to the play by Cornelius, who I know slightly and I think is taken with me? Well as I say, I was here to do this play "The Importance of Being Earnest" and Cornelius introduced me to the Professor. He had been asked to investigate a man who claimed to speak to the dead and I suggested that it would be dead easy for a woman to infiltrate a séance and he agreed. I thought it would be a fine jape, rather like playing a role on stage so I volunteered my services and now I want to learn more about the supernatural."

Well you've come to the right place," Evelyn felt relieved, for a very brief moment she thought there might be something between *her professor* and the petite *French* actress and it had made her realise how much she cared for him.

"Are you staying in Oxford, I have a spare room if you should need it?"

The two women had fallen into conversation when Guthridge reappeared to announce breathlessly. "Evie, I must return to London, there has been yet another death, it's one of the names on your list and what's more I've remembered where I've seen that word Golmi, it's from an old story about a thing made of clay to exact revenge at its builder's bidding, a thing more commonly known as a golem!"

Chapter Sixteen — Who is Adler?

Guthridge stood in the burnt-out ruin of the bakers shop with Inspector Poulson, both were watching Sidney Parret intently as he *read* the crime scene.

"He'd sent his wife and kids away for safety then set a trap for the creature and when it came for him he threw a load of oil and hot coals on it!" his eyes grew wide. "It were on fire and still it came. *"Damn you Adler"* he thought and he tried to push it back towards the ovens with his *peel* he did, but it were too strong, it smashed the bread paddle then smashed him, picked him up and chucked him in the oven!" the man staggered and Poulson came forward to support him. "His head were all broken, but he weren't properly dead you see?" his voice died to a whisper. "Oh lawd, he was put into that furnace still alive, gawd have mercy on his poor soul."

Guthridge tendered his hip-flask as before and the medium gratefully took it to drink deeply. "Well done Sidney, did you pick up anything else?"

"Yeah Prof, the baker got a good look at the damned thing, it were like a man but bigger, thicker, a bit like a thing a child might make out of clay. Its head was like an upturned bucket with a sort of face on it but just a slot where its mouth should be with glittering evil eyes above, like marbles they were and it were so big it could barely stand up in here and it was all on fire, but that didn't stop it!"

The policeman looked at the ceiling. "About ten feet tall, what do you reckon Arnold?"

"Yes Daniel, something like that" he replied then asked. "Sidney, was there anything written on that queer head?"

"Truth, it was written in them funny letters but he knew what it meant alright," replied Parret.

"Who is this Adler?" enquired the inspector.

"I didn't get that much, old bloke with a beard and one of them skullcaps like Jews wear, I think?" replied the clairvoyant.

"Someone wearing a kippa, did any of your men spot anyone like that hanging around the crime scene?" Guthridge asked Poulson.

"We're in Golders Green what do you think?" replied the policeman with a hint of sarcasm.

"Oh yes, of course, Sidney if I was to say golem what would it mean to you?"

The medium paled. "Golmi, it's written on the list of vengeance."

"Golmi, golem, what the deuce is that?" asked the Inspector.

"The Golmi or golem is a thing from Jewish folklore, a creature fashioned out of clay and brought to life to exact revenge" explained Guthridge. "Ticho, Meisel and no doubt that man from the river, all dead and all listed on the parchment. Then there's this fellow Adler, they must have done something wrong in the past and this creation is being used to settle the score." A look of alarm crossed the Professor's face. "Daniel, we have to find this Adler before the creature does!"

"That's if he's not already dead!" remarked Poulson.

"Well Mr. Parret, you've struck gold again, what was left of Meisel was found in the oven. He was little more than charred meat and bone, the skull had cracked open but the police surgeon couldn't determine if it wasn't down to the heat of the fire. Furthermore, a local down-and-out in the back alley swears he saw a smouldering giant emerge from the bakery to head in the direction of the river. He reeked of booze so the local police thought he was seeing things but I wasn't so certain and questioned the man myself, it looks like he wasn't far off the mark!"

"So what now Daniel?" asked the Professor.

"I need to interview a few more witnesses about this bearded chap, might find out something useful from one of them," he replied.

Chapter Seventeen – Schul is not Happy

"Look at the state of it!" shouted Schul. "I told you it wasn't ready to be sent out again!"

"How was I to know the bloody baker would set it on fire?" retorted Koen.

"It wasn't ready!" the holy man reiterated.

Their creation stood before them blackened and charred, large cracks were visible all over it, chunks of clay had fallen off in places and some of its fingers were missing, but the eyes still glittered.

Koen looked into the glassy balls. "I'd swear the damned thing's watching us."

"When the Shem is removed the golem becomes inactive, it does not possess a soul, it is merely a tool!" declared Schul confidently, he stepped up the ladder, took a charred piece of parchment from the mouth then held it out for Koen to see. "Oy look how badly burned the Shem is, that baker almost succeeded in stopping it dead.

"But he didn't and our golem returned unseen."

"God is still on our side it seems, so how is the other one progressing?" asked the rabbi shaking his head.

"Wallace says he will it have finished to be delivered

tomorrow" asserted the other.

"The goys are coming here, is that wise?" asked Schul.

"How else do we get it to the warehouse, walk it through the streets in broad daylight?"

"You could hire a van and bring it yourself?" returned the rabbi.

"All the easier to deal with them here, remember?" Koen reminded him of his plan. "And besides if you are so concerned over secrecy why did you show yourself to Adler last night?"

"I wanted to see him squirm and know that I was behind this, knowing that his was the last name on the list."

"Hmm, but it was a little foolhardy nonetheless."

"Who will he tell, who would believe him?" asked Schul. "Now back to the new golem, Joseph, I would much rather these workmen did not come here."

"As you wish my friend, it really doesn't matter where they die."

"They have done nothing to us, why must you kill them?" asked Schul.

"These things are sometimes necessary" replied his colleague coldly.

Schul had noticed a malicious gleam in Koen's eye of late and it worried him, not only that, seeing Adler's terrified look upon spotting him at the scene of the fire had not given the old man the satisfaction he'd sought. He was beginning to doubt himself and his comrade in arms more so.

Chapter Eighteen – Men are not all alike!

Evelyn, accompanied by her niece and Sally Miller, had journeyed to London with Guthridge and having spent the day sightseeing and shopping, ended their expedition at a fashionable restaurant near Liberty's where they arranged to meet the professor after he had dropped off Parret.

Guthridge, a little disconcerted at Mary's presence, related all that they learned at the crime scene and was in the middle of ordering food when the pompous Maître d'hôtel brought Poulson to them. "Inspector, you've timed it perfectly, would you care to order?"

The policeman felt a little intimidated by the opulent surroundings. "Oh, I er don't know?"

"Oh please do Inspector, it's my treat, I can well afford it" insisted Mary, who as Lord Theddingworth's wife had a considerable allowance.

"Thank you, milady," Poulson would have doffed his hat if he hadn't already removed it!

Mary laughed lightly. "Oh, Inspector Poulson you are far too polite, no-one addresses me in that way. Lady Mary will suffice until we know each other better."

Poulson sat at the table to order a fillet and potatoes from the hovering waiter then turned to speak quietly to Guthridge. "Arnold, I need to speak to you about an important discovery, in private."

"You need have no concern in speaking openly here Daniel both Evelyn and Sally have been of great service to my investigations in the past and *Lady* Mary is, I'm sure, the very soul of discretion."

"Very well Arnold, one of the bystanders remembers seeing a familiar figure in the crowd who seemed quite disturbed by the fire. A rabbi by the name of Goldman *and* the baker used to attend his synagogue."

"Well, he may have known Meisel as a friend?" suggested the professor.

"I've already crossed paths with this Goldman, remember? He was the one who muttered a prayer under his breath and claimed not to able to understand the parchment. I suspected he was dodgy at the time!"

"The name on the list is Adler, but I suppose he could have changed it?" Evie mused aloud.

"Quite!" said Poulson abruptly. "Tomorrow the rabbi is going to be receiving another visit from Scotland Yard, would you care to accompany me, Arnold?"

"It's not going to help us find this golem though is it?" ventured Guthridge.

"No, but if he is Adler he may know who would want him dead. If the thing's still in working order that is, Bill Simms, the vagrant who saw it says it was limping badly as it stomped away. Meisel seems to at least have done it some damage before he died!" replied the policeman.

"It will have returned to its creator who will doubtless be repairing it as we speak," stated the professor. "And that will require a lot of clay if I'm right about this?"

"You'll need to find out who has been ordering large quantities of clay recently." piped up Evelyn.

"Madam, please, this is police business!" said Poulson.

"A local builder's merchants would be a good place to

start looking and that might give you a clue as to who he is," she continued unabashed.

"Him?" asked the inspector, a little peeved.

"Well yes, I couldn't see a woman doing something as dreadful as this, could you?" she replied, smiling sweetly.

"Miss Poole, as grateful as I am for your *helpful* advice, these people often tend to be quite insular and very reluctant to discuss their business with outsiders. May I be as bold as to suggest that this is best left to the *men* who are dealing with the investigation?" he was getting a little annoyed at this woman advising him on what he should be doing.

"Do you have no women at Scotland Yard?" she retorted frostily.

"I am proud to say we have a dozen in our employ, they deal with children and look after female prisoners."

"Not in any crime solving capacity then?" Evelyn was not letting it go.

"My dear Miss Poole, gentle ladies such as yourselves would find the rigours of police work too stressful and demanding I am sure." he replied.

"Ahem yes, Daniel erm," Guthridge could see the women beginning to seethe.

"Pah!" exclaimed Sally. "I grew up in Whitechapel next door to a bawdy house and cleaned there as a child when that murderer was killing them poor whores. I learned to read and write and was lucky enough to better my circumstances, so do not think to tell me what I would find rigorous or stressful!" Sally did not mention having worked at the same establishment in a different capacity when of age while bettering her circumstances.

"Bravo!" cried Evelyn. "You men have no idea what it is like to live as a second-class citizen in your own country!"

"Evelyn please, we *men* are not all alike!" started the professor.

"Forgive me, Arnold, you are the exception to the

rule," she replied.

"I apologise if I have upset you ladies, may I assure you nothing was further from my intention," asserted Poulson with more contrition than he actually felt.

Evelyn's niece spoke up. "Ladies, gentlemen, could we please calm ourselves and be as friends, this bizarre business should take precedence for the moment whatever our feelings regarding the inequality of the sexes. Now let us enjoy this excellent repast that the waiters desire to bring to our table."

"Very well said Mary," affirmed Evelyn. "We could help you on the quiet?" she whispered to Guthridge.

"My dear, it could be very dangerous, I would rather you did not," he replied.

"The answer is definitely no!" stated Poulson, who had overheard.

Evelyn smiled and acquiesced while thinking, *we'll see about that!*

"Couldn't we help in some small way?" asked Mary after they had dined.

"Lady Mary, I must apologise once again but I remain unmoved with respect to your involvement in the investigation," returned Poulson.

She fixed him with a stare. "My dear Inspector, if we were to visit some of these builder's merchants as suggested by my aunt, might they not be more amenable to revealing their confidentialities to "the fairer sex", as you might put it?"

"Oh, err I'm not sure if that's wise?" Poulson didn't know if it was the excellent wine or the feeling of well-being from his meal but his will was weakening under the young woman's blue-eyed gaze. "They tend to be rather rough types, not the sort you'd want to mix with."

"Inspector, I find men to be either courteous or lecherous. If they are the former it will not be a problem, if they are the latter, well, I have a pistol and Miss Miller seems quite a formidable sort. I believe we would have little problem!" declared Evelyn.

Mary kept her eyes steadily fixed on Poulson's. "My aunt is correct. It's not as if we're going after the miscreants ourselves, we would merely be helping you track them down."

"Well, my men are quite stretched and it could be of help but you must avoid confrontation at all costs," the policeman couldn't believe he was agreeing to this.

"Then we start first thing in the morning!" stated Evelyn firmly.

"Yes, but you are to contact a police officer the moment you discover anything," said Poulson somewhat vaguely.

"You have my word on it!" Mary assured him before breaking her concentration.

Guthridge chuckled to himself, only too aware of what had just been done.

CHAPTER NINETEEN – ADLER

Rabbi Goldman went to the front door and peered warily through the spyhole to see the police inspector from the other day standing there with a scholarly looking man dressed in tweed and sporting a large sandy moustache.

Somewhat relieved, Goldman pocketed the pistol he was carrying and opened it to greet them. "Shalom, Inspector, it is something of a surprise to see you again?"

"Yes sir, we're following a new line of enquiry and this is my esteemed colleague, Professor Guthridge of St Aidan's College, Oxford."

"Shalom, Rabbi Goldman" Guthridge extended his hand and the holy man shook it cautiously.

"St Aidan's, you must forgive me for I am not familiar with the college, are you not a little far from home Professor?"

"He is an expert in his field Rabbi and that is why I have brought him with me" answered Poulson.

"And what may I ask is that, Professor?"

"I have many fields of study but you might say I specialise in the arcane and the uncanny" replied Guthridge.

"At the moment my specific interest is in the mysteries of the Kabala."

Goldman paled slightly. "Now I understand why you might seek my advice but I could help you very little there, it is not something a simple rabbi would have knowledge of."

"Really?" asked Poulson. "Fair enough, but what we're here for is to ask what you know about the fire at the baker's last night?"

Goldman tried to hide his nervousness. "A dreadful business, I knew the man, Meisel I think he was?"

"Rudolph Meisel was his name," stated Poulson.

"Yes, yes that was him, oy what a terrible thing to happen to a man."

"One of your parishioners perchance?" continued the policeman.

"Yes, he did worship here on occasion, he was a family man I have said a prayer for him and his poor wife?"

"Did you know an Aaron Bergman?"

"I believe he was a friend of Meisel's." answered Goldman, clearly on edge.

"And Franz Ticho?" asked Poulson.

"The goldsmith?" responded the rabbi. "Only by reputation, it is not a thing a man of God should say but he was a worthless crazy piece of shit, a meshuggener!"

"What if I told you someone had identified you as a man called Adler?"

"What nonsense is this, I am Samuel Goldman?"

"You could easily have changed your name?" suggested Poulson.

"Why would I want to do such a thing?" snapped the rabbi.

"To hide from someone seeking revenge, perhaps?" continued the policeman.

Goldman drew his pistol to point it at Poulson. "How can you know that?"

"The Golmi will punish him last!" stated Guthridge

suddenly.

"What?" the cleric turned to him in shock and Poulson, seizing his chance, wrested the weapon from his hand.

"Right then, we'll discuss this down at the station!" said the policeman firmly, turning the gun on *Goldman*.

* * *

Samuel Adler now in custody, sat at a table facing Poulson and Guthridge, who had been allowed to attend the interview. "You know of the Golmi?" he asked the professor.

"Yes, we deciphered one of the parchments Rabbi Adler, we know all about the golem and its purpose."

The holy shrugged in resignation. "Ah yes, sent to make us suffer by informing us of our impending and inevitable doom and I, the last on the list must suffer the most. Meisel believed fire could destroy it but he was wrong, I am as doomed as they all were. It seems God does not want to forgive us."

"But it can be stopped, according to the Story of the Golem of Prague one has merely to remove the Shem from its mouth, is that not correct?" asked the professor.

"Oy vey, simply remove the Shem from its mouth, while at the same time you are being crushed or torn apart by a giant monster of clay!" replied the rabbi sardonically.

"There is no other way?" inquired Poulson.

"Not that I have found in Loew's book and believe me I have searched thoroughly, impending demise at the hands of the Golmi makes a man very eager to find a way."

"You're safe in police custody, the bloody thing can't get to you here!" affirmed the inspector and the old man laughed bitterly in response.

"You have a copy of the Kabala of Judah Loew?" asked Guthridge excitedly. "Might I see it?"

Goldman shrugged. "I cannot stop you, it's at my home but it will do you little good."

"Why is this creation being sent after you, after all of you?" demanded the policeman.

"It all started in Prague a decade hence, our once proud Bohemia had been absorbed by the Austro-Hungarian Empire and after twenty years under the yoke of the oppressors the people were unhappy, we Jews most of all, insurgency was rife throughout the land, some were determined to restore the Kingdom of Bohemia while others sought government by the masses. I was one of the latter and with a group of like-minded individuals formed the "Hand of God", each of us was a *finger*, each with our band of angry young men. A man called Joseph Koen was our *thumb*, the organiser, he was charismatic clever and brilliant. Unfortunately he was also a half-crazed zealot and under his direction we carried out several bloody strikes against the empire, even derailing a troop train on its way to the city."

"I remember reading about that in the newspapers, a lot of women and children died as I recall!" remarked Poulson.

"Yes, we were unaware their families were travelling with them, now God has returned to me I bitterly regret my part in it but alas I cannot turn back the clock."

"You still haven't explained why there is a golem pursuing you" remarked Guthridge.

"Or what Bohemian insurgents are doing in England?" interjected the policeman.

"The four of us were betrayed for money and interrogated brutally. The police wanted to know where Koen was hiding and gave us a choice, freedom or imprisonment in Pankrác prison and it is not a nice place. They cleverly put us in the same cell to discuss what had been offered, I am not the stuff of which martyrs are made and quickly persuaded Meisel and Bergman but Ticho, always the hard man, bickered and blustered until finally giving in. The fingers of the *hand* betrayed the thumb and fearing vengeance from his many supporters we fled as far as Lon-

Chapter Twenty – A Plan Comes Unstuck

"**H**ello, we're collecting on behalf of the St Nicholas Foundation for Fallen Women" announced Evie, thrusting forward a wooden box.

"Never heard of yer?" replied the man at the door, his overall was covered in spots and splashes of clay.

"Oh we're a very new charity aren't we, Sister Mary?" continued the woman.

"That we are Sister Evelyn and I'm sure such a fine gentleman as you could spare a few shillings for poor unfortunate women who have fallen on hard times," replied one of the others.

Harry Snodgrass regarded the trio, they were well turned out but not too extravagantly dressed (Sarah had insisted they didn't stand out too much), the one called Mary was looking right into his eyes, right into his head… "Well I haven't got any lucre on me I'll have to get some off the gaffer."

"That's lovely of you," said the older woman pushing her way past him. They had visited several builders' merchants in the guise of charity collectors using Mary's skill at mesmerism to ensure the proprietors were co-operative. The sixth had turned up trumps, a small firm by the name of Bankside Artisans had been ordering huge quantities of potter's clay recently and when the merchant inquired why he had been given an evasive answer about garden ornaments. The women decided they would follow this new lead themselves and inform Poulson later.

"Erm I'm not sure Mr. Wallace would like you doing that, it ain't really safe in there, for women that is!" he cried.

"Don't be so silly, we are quite sensible!" said the third pushing past him.

"Hello ladies, what can I do for you?" asked a dark bearded man in a voice redolent of Eastern Europe. He was standing on the stairs to the office and had no clay on his smart suit.

"We are collecting for the St Nicholas Foundation for Fallen Woman," reiterated Evelyn casting her eyes around the workshop with its kilns and stacks of moulds.

The man smiled insincerely. "A worthy cause I'm sure, Snodgrass, please give these delightful ladies five shillings from the cash box."

"You can't throw the boss's money around like that, where is he anyway?" asked the younger man.

"He is indisposed, just give these fine ladies some money and let them go on their way."

"Oh you are not the proprietor then?" asked Evie curiously, on one side of the workshop she could see a large cart, its cargo covered by a tarpaulin.

"No, I am his business partner, does that matter to you?" asked the man suspiciously.

"No!" replied Evie a little too sharply, she moved her hand close to her handbag. "If our small request is going to cause an argument between you and this young man, we will take our leave, thank you."

Koen, noticing Mary had wandered across the workshop in an attempt to scrutinise the cart's covered cargo, produced a pistol. "Regrettably I think you must stay."

Evelyn had drawn her own weapon and levelled it at him. "I rather think otherwise, Mary, Sally get to the door!"

"They came to rob your boss, Snodgrass, do something you fool!" lied Koen.

Sally produced a lethal looking stiletto from her boot and grabbing the unfortunate Snodgrass held it to his throat. "One wrong move mister and your friend gets his throat opened!"

Koen, laughing harshly, trained his gun on Evie. "Let's see if you have it in you to pull the trigger!"

Evelyn had and fired first intending only to wound but missed Koen who flinched as her bullet sang past causing him to shoot wide and his bullet ricocheted off one of the kilns to strike Mary in the centre of the chest.

"Auntie!" she gasped wide-eyed as a bright red bloom spread across the front of her blouse, she sank to her knees then to the floor, seemingly lifeless.

"You bastard!" yelled Evie firing wildly while backing towards the wall as she tried to reach her niece prone on the floor.

Koen fired several quick shots in response then took steady aim.

Sally gasped in horror as she saw Evie stagger back, blood running down her face, to fall heavily against one of the large casement windows which, being in poor repair broke under the impact to pitch the stricken woman into the water below. "You fucker!" she screamed holding her blade under Harry's chin while backing towards the door. "Your friend is a dead man!"

Koen, unflustered, walked steadily towards the couple.

"Mr. Cohen, stay back, she'll kill me for sure!" wailed Snodgrass.

For an answer Koen sneered and coldly shot the unfortunate man in the head.

"Back off or I'll cut your balls off!" cried a shocked and blood-spattered Sally, holding her point towards him.

"Put the knife down girl, I will not kill a woman as pretty as you without good reason."

"You killed my friends!" she snarled.

He regarded Mary's prostrate form on the floor then the broken window. "That one was a regrettable accident and the other was trying to take my life, any jury would acknowledge I was defending myself. Put the blade down or I will shoot you where you stand!"

Trembling with fear the young actress dropped the stiletto to the floor only for Koen to step forward and knock her out with a single blow.

When Koen had harnessed horses to the cart and driven off with the unconscious actress aboard, Mary opened her eyes, rolled over and sat up to look around cautiously. She reached inside her blouse to remove the still warm, bloodstained bullet that had been expelled from her chest. *That bloody hurt, I didn't expect my immortality to be tested quite so soon!*

Staggering to the window on shaky legs, Mary looked out over the water but could see no sign of her aunt. The ricochet had stopped her heart and at first she lay unable to move but as her body recovered, had managed to remain still with the bullet burning in her chest in the vain hope of turning her *death* to advantage. When the fusillade of shots ended with the crash of breaking glass, she surmised what had happened then the conversation between Koen and Sally confirmed her aunt's apparent demise. Still in some pain Mary half staggered from the workshop to see the cart disappearing around the corner scattering aside curious folk who had been drawn by the commotion, *she must find Professor Guthridge!*

"Excuse me Miss are you alright?" asked a police constable emerging from the sizeable crowd that was gathering.

"There is a woman in the river, you must find her!"

screamed Mary.

* * *

Albert Moggs spotted the body in the water then after catching its clothing with a boat hook pulled the limp form onto his boat. "Mabel, we've got ourselves a floater."

"Anything worth having on it, Bert?" came a woman's voice from the stern.

Moggs turned the body over and it coughed up water. "Shit me if she ain't still alive?"

"Let's have a look?" asked Moggs' wife coming along the boat. "Bloody hell she's been bashed on the head."

Mr. Moggs examined the wound. "No Mabel, I've seen this before when I was in Africa fighting them Boers, it's what they call a glancing shot. Someone's tried to kill her with a gun!"

"Let's get you sat up!" said his wife gently putting a meaty arm around the woman, who coughed again and opened her eyes briefly before fainting away. "Get her some brandy then set off for the quay, Bert, we need to find ourselves a Bobbie, there might be some reward in this.

Chapter Twenty One – Sally in Trouble

Sally opened her eyes to find herself tied to a chair in a darkened room, her head was pounding and she had a split lip, but at least she was still alive. "Help!" she screamed at the top of her voice. "Help… help… murder!"

A door opened and a dim light shone into the room. "Shut up little girl, no-one can hear you here."

Sally glared at the outline silhouetted against the door. "You don't frighten me, you cunt!"

"Then you are as foolish as you are foul mouthed, girl!" retorted the man.

Another voice came from outside the door in a language she didn't understand.

"Why didn't you leave her at the workshop, why bring her here?" asked Schul.

"This pretty little thing may know something of what we're doing and will be useful if we need a hostage." answered Koen.

Schul grunted acknowledgement then asked. "How many died?"

"Four" Koen related the events at Bankside Artisans.

"Oy vey and they were all gentiles?" Schul noticed his colleague's eyes had that maniacal glint again. It occurred to him that Joseph often had that look and somehow he'd never noticed before or had perhaps denied it to himself.

"Yes what of it?"

"The police will redouble their efforts now, especially since two of them were women!"

"I had no choice, Isaac."

"No choice? Violence seems to come so naturally to you, this must be over soon we need to leave at the earliest opportunity."

"What happened to your famous patience?" sneered Koen.

"You did!" snapped Schul in reply.

"Well, send the golem for Adler then we can leave."

"The police have him in custody! I watched them take him away, that Inspector, the one who has been all over Golders Green since Ticho's death and a man who looked like a teacher."

"Then send the original golem to attack the police station and if it's destroyed killing him who cares?"

"I can't, the police have someone very clever working on their side and they keep moving the bastard around making it nigh on impossible to locate him using a seeking tract and he is the one I want, the others didn't matter to me!"

"But you agreed to leave him to last, letting him sweat while watching the others die first?" retorted Koen petulantly.

"A mistake in hindsight, I had expected things to run more smoothly."

They both regarded Miller who was glaring at the pair silhouetted in the doorway. "Do you think she knows where Adler is?" asked Schul.

"We need to find out who she is and who her friends were working for, I could work on her but I admit to being somewhat reluctant to hurt such a pretty, is there some

Kabbalistic magic that would make her talk?"

"Do you think the Hungarians could be behind this?" asked the old man.

"They all appeared to be English but it is a possibility. Adler was not behind this though, I am certain of it. Isaac, do you have anything you can use?"

"I believe I do, I'll need to write the tract tonight."

Koen looked into the room and grinned. "You'd better get a good night's sleep little girl, you have an interesting day ahead of you tomorrow."

Chapter Twenty Two – Pulled from the Water

Clarence Wallace the ex-proprietor of Bankside Artisans had been discovered in his mezzanine office, throat cut from ear to ear and Harold Snodgrass, the only worker retained when trade had slumped, was found in the workshop shot through the head. The inspector waited respectfully while the bodies were stretchered to a police ambulance for transport to the mortuary, there were no parchments or crushed heads this time, their deaths by pistol and knife seemed almost mundane by comparison *and* thinking on what Guthridge suggested he'd had the place dusted for fingerprints.

He watched as the wagon was driven off, *why didn't those damned women listen to him yesterday?* He examined the curious bloodstain in the middle of the floor that bore impressions of what looked like buttons, almost as if someone had lain in it then crossed to the broken window, there by the shattered casement was the Webley .455 dropped by Evelyn as she fell along with several spent casings, the only indication of her presence. The inspector had earlier turned away a distraught Guthridge, suggesting he join the niece at her posh hotel.

Poulson glumly regarded the waters of the Brent as they flowed past outside, Evelyn Poole's body would have been washed downstream to the Thames by now. He had sent a police boat out to search the river but held little hope of finding her alive, according to Lady Mary, she had been shot in the head before falling through the window, *she must be a cool customer that woman, laying doggo in the middle of a gun battle.!* Poulson was very curious to know how her ladyship had managed to come out unscathed from what must have been a fierce exchange of fire, even more curious was the report from the constable who had arrived on the scene first who stated that judging by her apparel, he believed her to have been shot in the chest.

His musing was broken by Sergeant Thicke rushing into the workshop to breathlessly report. "It's Miss Poole, sir, she's been found alive. A boatman pulled her out of the water an hour ago!"

***

Evelyn came to with a splitting headache and gingerly reached to touch her bandaged head. "Evie thank God you're alive!" said a familiar voice, Guthridge having ensured she had a private room, had kept vigil by her bed for several hours.

"Oh, Arnold, this is all my fault!" declared the woman.

"No Evie it is not!"

"Of course it is, that idiot Poulson wound me up so much with his male arrogance that I decided the three of us would be a match for the police. I know poor Mary was struck by a stray bullet but what happened to Sally?"

"Miss Miller was taken prisoner by Koen and your niece is alive and surprisingly unharmed. She has told me everything that happened, except of course how she was able to take a bullet to the chest and survive?"

"We had better leave that one for another day, Arnold. But what of Sally, do you know where she is being held?" asked Evelyn, relieved to hear confirmation of her niece's immortality.

"Sadly not and don't blame yourself for what happened, I'm sure this radical would have put up as much of a fight if he had been faced by the whole of Scotland Yard itself. At least you were armed, a police truncheon is not much of a weapon against a bullet" Guthridge assured her. "And I can think of no-one more capable than you, my dear."

"Thank you Arnold you are, as always, a comfort to me, now where is Mary?"

"I'm afraid she is being what I think they call, grilled, by Inspector Poulson as we speak, I'm going to pick up Sidney shortly and we are going to visit the crime scene with him."

"Arnold, thank you for being here when I woke up," Evie took his hand gently.

"It was nothing my dear, I would wait forever for you."

"Arnold, I..." but before a misty-eyed Evelyn could finish her sentence a nurse entered the room to check on her patient.

A smart, moustachioed young officer had followed her in. "What ho, sis, I heard about what happened so I thought I'd pop over and visit you!" he declared brightly. The soldier was dressed in the drab khaki that was beginning to replace the familiar scarlet tunic of the British Army.

"Algy, how nice to see you!" said Evie. "Arnold, I don't believe you have met my younger brother, have you?"

"So you're the old fossil Evelyn has taken up with, eh?" the young officer shook his hand firmly. "Lieutenant Algernon Poole at your service sir, so, why haven't you made a decent woman of my sister yet, eh?"

"Err?" Guthridge was nonplussed.

"Algy, behave yourself!" snapped Evelyn. "Arnold take no notice of the idiot, he does like to tease!"

"No harm meant old chap, my sister Evie's a tough old boot, no doubt told you she wasn't the marrying kind, eh?" the officer returned with a friendly grin.

"Algy, for goodness sake!" cried his sister in vexation.

"Ma'am if you are going to get upset I shall have to insist these gentleman leave!" cautioned the nurse.

"Err, I'd better go and find Sidney, I'll be back later" announced Guthridge a little nonplussed.

Evie wistfully watched him leave while her dressing was being checked, then turned to her brother to ask. "So Algy why are you in London, I thought you were stationed in Salisbury?"

"My unit's at the Tower, sis, learning all about a new mark of the Maxim gun..." Guthridge heard her brother explain as he descended the stairs.

* * *

Over at Scotland Yard, Poulson was becoming incensed. "Pardon my language Lady Theddingworth but what were you bloody well thinking? Miss Poole is in hospital and we have no idea of the whereabouts of Miss Miller," he stated in exasperation. "Why, why did you not just tell us what you had found out, we would have flooded the area with policemen, we could have caught this Koen villain red-handed!"

"If we had waited for you the man would have gone by the time you got there, at least we now know what he looks like," replied Mary somewhat contritely

"But at what cost?" snapped the inspector angrily.

"I say, Poulson that will do!" Lord William had trav-elled to London and insisted on being present. "My wife has had quite enough trouble for now. I am travelling to Italy shortly and insist that she return to Pendleberry with me on the next train!"

"William, I am capable of looking after myself," she assured him haughtily. "Inspector Poulson, you are quite correct it *was* a foolhardy venture on our part and William, I insist upon my staying in London until my aunt has recovered and poor Sally has been found."

Lord William harrumphed, knowing he was beaten.

Poulson suppressed a wry smile, *she's definitely related to Evelyn Poole.* "Thank you, Lady Theddingworth, I have your statement so you may go for now" he nodded courteously to the Lord as he bade him farewell then stared after the couple as they departed, *she had a bloodstained bullet hole smack bang in the middle of her blouse when the constable found her yet was completely unharmed, how is that possible? I suppose I shouldn't be too surprised, she is part of Guthridge's circle and he has a knack for attracting the weird and wonderful.*

There was a knock at the door and on being acknowledged a constable entered his office to inform him. "Inspector, there's two gentlemen to see you, sir, a Professor Guthridge and a weaselly bloke called Parret?"

"About bloody time!" said Poulson.

CHAPTER TWENTY THREE – THE TRACT OF EMET

"Come girl, wake up!" said a voice.

Sarah blearily opened her eyes, she had been given a rough cot in the attic of the warehouse and heard the men talking late into the night but had been unable to understand anything they said. As her vision cleared she saw the voice belonged to Koen, the man who had taken her prisoner.

He thrust a mug of tea at her. "No breakfast?" she asked brightly, sitting up and taking it while trying to mask her inner fear.

"What?" he growled.

"This is not a nice way to treat a lady."

"You are a brave young woman, you would have made a good recruit for the Hand, I think."

"You are quite wrong, sir, I disapprove of anarchists!"

"I am no anarchist, I merely believe in my country's freedom!" snapped Koen.

"I understand your desire for liberation, but it seems you believe in retribution far more?" retorted the actress.

"You have no idea what you are talking about!"

"You are killing people for revenge here in London

when you should be fighting for your precious freedom in Bohemia."

Koen grabbed her face with one rough hand and stared into it. "You seem to know a lot about me, girl, but you have no idea what damage those traitors did!" Koen tightened his grip and pushed her onto the bed raising his free hand in a fist. "How much do you know, I wonder?"

"Bastard!" she mumbled through his hand, eyes wide in terror.

Koen unclenched his fist then ran his hand familiarly over her body before releasing his grip and standing back from the cot. "It is lucky for you I am a decent man."

"What are you going to do to me?" her bravura had faded and she was shaking visibly.

"Don't worry girl I won't spoil your pretty face as long as you behave yourself, get up and follow me." Koen led her down to the ground floor of the building where the chair awaited her once more.

Once bound, Sally cast her eyes around to see a large figure stood in shadow in the corner. It was blackened and charred, fresh clay stood out redly on its darkened surface but despite the damage it was still formidable to behold. "Is that your golem?" she asked nervously.

"My, but you do know a lot about us little girl and now we are going find out exactly how much" Koen informed her.

Schul appeared from another door and walked up to her. "Who are you?" asked Sally.

The rabbi merely smiled and held a piece of paper towards her while Koen held her head tightly, forcing her to look at it. On the paper was a diagram consisting of ten circles in a roughly rectangular pattern linked by straight lines and each had a single symbol inside it. Unbeknown to Sally they were letters in Hebrew, written in a sequence designed to elicit a specific response.

"Do you know what the word "emet" means?" asked Koen, close by her ear.

"No?" she replied, the rabbi began to chant and the symbols seemed to shake in their circular prisons.

"It means truth, little girl, soon all your secrets will be ours!" exclaimed Koen.

The letters appeared to break free of the paper and hover before her eyes to move about in a strange pattern, gaining momentum as Schul's chanting began to eat its way into her mind.

She woke once more upon the rough cot to see Koen framed in the open doorway watching her fervently and it made her feel very uncomfortable.

"Thank you Sally, you have been very forthcoming" he said on seeing her awake. The door closed, leaving the young woman alone with no idea of what had happened.

Chapter Twenty four – A Lead from a Pencil

The premises of Bankside Artisans had seen better times, situated on the east side of the Brent it had once employed over twenty craftsmen and apprentices, now three men stood in the office of its former proprietor overlooking what had once been a busy workshop.

Guthridge was taking in the extensive bloodstain spread across the desk and floor as Parret *read* the room. "He killed the boss, he had come to discuss transporting something to his warehouse, then he took the bloke by surprise and slit his throat straight across, Harry didn't know about it cos' he was downstairs answering the door, then the three women came saying they was collecting for charity."

"We know most of this this already, Parret." the policeman complained.

"Well, after her Ladyship got shot and Miss Poole went out the window…" started the medium.

"Lady Mary did get shot, I knew it!" exclaimed Poulson triumphantly.

"No, I meant pretended to get shot," Sidney had caught Guthridge's anxious look. "He came down the stairs and shot poor old Harold in the head, leaving Sally with only her stiletto to fight him with!"

"She had a stiletto?" asked the inspector in surprise.

"Sally had alluded to a rather colourful upbringing, Daniel, if you care to recall?" Guthridge reminded him.

"Yeah, she was threating to use it on Harold but the bearded fella didn't give a stuff, he's a nasty one that bloke and no mistake!" continued the clairvoyant.

"Do you know what happened to her?" asked Poulson.

"Sorry Inspector there ain't nothing after that."

"Knife wielding actresses, bulletproof aristocrats and your gun-toting lady friend, what strange company you do keep Arnold!" remarked Poulson sardonically. "So Sidney, anything else we might not know?"

"The man, they called him Cohen, asked them to build a big statue out of clay, said it was a special commission for an exhibition. He offered plenty of money and Mr. Wallace, who was broke, seized on the opportunity. This Cohen seemed an alright sort of geezer, he paid up front for materials and was smiling right up to when he took a razor to the poor sod's throat," he shuddered. "That's the bit I hate most, seeing the poor buggers getting topped from their vantage point like, shakes up the nerves something bad, I could do with something to calm 'em?" hinted the medium.

On cue, Guthridge handed him his hip flask. "You're doing very well Sidney, can you see if Wallace had an address for this Cohen?"

"It was in his ledger, like all his customer's addresses" replied Parret.

"That's no help I'm afraid, someone tore the most recent page from it and given the state of Wallace's business I would say Cohen's was the only address on it" stated Poulson.

"Daniel is the ledger still here?" asked the professor.

"You're in luck, it has been dusted for prints but it's

still here" Poulson opened a filing cabinet and removed a large ledger, opening it to show the page torn out. "Only Wallace and another, as yet, unidentified individual have handled it recently.

Guthridge took it and held it up to catch the sunlight streaming through the windowpane. "Ah, I hoped that there might be an impression from the page above, but it is quite difficult to see" Guthridge paused. "Do you have a pencil by any chance?" Poulson found one and handed it to the professor. "Daniel do, I have your permission to deface this book?"

"I'm ahead of you already, Arnold, scribble away!" he replied and they watched as Guthridge gently shaded over the slight impression to reveal a few scattered letters exposed in hollow relief where Wallace had pressed hard with his pen nib.

Poulson pursed his lips and pulled at his moustache in contemplation. "Not a lot to go on I'm afraid, I can make out a "Coh", that will be Cohen no doubt and "da Ro.., Hanwell", we'll need a list of the streets around there?"

"Don't need one Inspector!" announced Parret, there's a bloke talks to me occasionally who worked on the canal there fifty years ago. We often discuss the old times and there's only two streets in Hanwell ending in da, Hilda Road runs almost parallel to the canal and Saint Ada Row tees off it, goes right down to the towpath."

"Are you talking about someone who is dead by any chance?" asked Guthridge.

"Passed over, if you please Prof. his name's Benny, don't know his last name. Likes to visit every now and then, nice bloke, fell off his boat and got crushed against the lock side while it were filling up."

"Ye Gods!" exclaimed Poulson.

"Come on Inspector, I was spot on about the other stuff weren't I?" grinned the clairvoyant.

Poulson shrugged in resignation. "Very well, I'll get a message to the local police station and get them to make a few discrete enquiries."

CHAPTER TWENTY FIVE – SCHUL IS WORRIED

Sally regarded the plate of cheese and black bread Schul was holding with suspicion. "Do you expect me to eat this shit?" her defiant streak had returned.

"You're very impudent considering your situation and this is all you'll be getting, food is provided by the Lord merely to sustain the body" the old man replied in his broken English. Having become concerned that Koen was developing an unnatural interest in their prisoner, Schul had taken over looking after her.

She reluctantly took the plate along with the tin mug of tea he was proffering. "What will you do with me now?"

"You will remain our hostage until we are ready to leave and I promise you will not be harmed *unless* you give good reason" with that Schul left, locking her in the attic room.

"How is our guest?" asked Koen when the old rabbi joined him.

"Churlish as ever" replied Schul.

"She has chutzpah that girl and is easy on the eye too" remarked Koen with a grin that made the older man uneasy.

"We have more pressing issues to consider than how pretty our hostage is. We need to discover Adler's whereabouts, that's far more important."

"Well, we know the name of this professor helping the police, perhaps he could be convinced to *assist* us in finding the traitor or one of his associates maybe?" suggested Koen.

"It is an idea and we know where he is staying, that would be a good place to start."

Koen took out his pistol and checked it making Schul nervous, he smiled grimly. "Don't worry Isaac, I'm just going to see what he looks like, perhaps follow him and check what he gets up to."

"Oy, Joseph please keep your temper in check and don't cause any more trouble, we have enough than we can handle as it is."

"You know me Isaac."

"And that is why I worry Joseph."

Professor Guthridge returned to the hospital that evening to find Evelyn well on the way to recovery and hoping to be discharged tomorrow with the doctor's agreement. After spending an hour with her talking over old adventures Arnold bid her a fond farewell and was pleasantly surprised when she kissed him goodnight.

Once outside, he hailed a Hansom cab to take him back to his hotel and on boarding the vehicle spotted someone lurking in the shadows on the other side of the street. "Hullo?" he called but the figure walked briskly off, *that was odd?*

Koen cursed under his breath, *he was getting careless the goy had seen him!* He wasn't too worried about the scholarly looking professor but the obvious policeman in plain clothes standing guard at the hospital door and very likely armed, did give him some cause for concern.

When he returned to the warehouse Schul had moved his camp-bed next to the stairs to the upper room. *Did Isaac believe he had designs on the shiksa?* He stared at the attic door for a while, his thoughts on the attractive young woman locked up there. "Do you think I cannot control my desires, stupid old fool!" he muttered under his breath.

Schul watched through slitted eyelids as his compatriot skulked off to find his bed, *the sooner this was over and done with, the better!*

Koen tried to sleep but could not get the actress out of his thoughts or her previous profession and when he was certain the old man was in a deep sleep, removed his shoes to tread carefully and quietly up the stairs.

Chapter Twenty Six – Broken Conspiracy

Koen began patching up the original golem as soon as dawn broke while Schul created another seeking tract and succeeded in locating their prey at a police station not a mile distant. Once the clay giant had been repaired as best as possible in the short time they had, it would be sent on a one-way mission before the police moved him again, kill Adler or Goldman as he called himself and anyone who stood in its way.

Finally satisfied that sufficient work had been done Schul sat down to meticulously write the new Shem. He looked up to see Koen bringing a tray to the desk. "Only two cups Joseph, what about our hostage?"

"Let the little bitch stew, we've treated her like a princess for long enough." he retorted.

Isaac, noticing a scratch on his cheek asked. "Did you catch yourself on something when you were working on the Golmi, Joseph?"

"Yes, stupid of me" he grinned.

The old man narrowed his eyes. "Well, I think I'll take her my cup and make a fresh one for myself when I come down."

"Suit yourself, Isaac, is the Shem finished?"

"Nearly" Schul lied as he climbed the stairs.

He opened the door to the attic to find Sally huddled in a corner of the room wrapped in a coarse blanket. She raised hate-filled eyes to him. "Come for your turn, have you?"

The old man's heart sank as he saw the torn clothing scattered on the bed and realised what had occurred. "Oy, what has the bastard done?" he felt sick. "My dear girl, please forgive me for allowing this to happen."

Sally said nothing but just stared at the floor.

"Girl" he whispered. "When I leave the door will be left unlocked. On the floor below this there is a stairway which leads to the canal towpath and the door it is only bolted on this side. Do you understand what I'm telling you?"

She nodded and mouthed *thank you* by way of reply.

"Koen where are you?" shouted Schul as he descended the steps gun in hand, the man appeared from the stairs to the ground floor. "Why, why did you have to lower yourself to that?" he demanded angrily.

"Why are you so bothered? The shiksa is still alive isn't she, is she upset because she didn't receive payment?"

"*She* is a frightened young woman!"

"You're taking the side of an ex-harlot Isaac, that's rich?"

"No woman deserves that, have you taken leave of your senses?"

"She would have happily led the police right to us, her and her friends!" the mad glint was in his eye again. "Have you forgotten what she told us, what they were doing at that fool Wallace's?"

"This is not what we are, it's not part of the cause, first all the unnecessary killing and now this, do you have an iota of compassion in you?"

"You can talk old man, what's happened to your desire for vengeance?"

"I wanted revenge on those who betrayed us, I wanted revenge on the empire not this, not innocent people! Joseph what's happened to you, I feel I can't trust you anymore?"

"You can't trust me? You lied to me old man, the Shem is complete!" Koen had been very attentive to the rabbi's teaching and had deciphered the script for himself. "I don't think I need you any longer!"

"Oh really, try writing one you meshuggener!" Schul raised his pistol but Koen fired first and the old man tumbled down the wooden stairs to lay motionless upon the floor. Somewhere outside a horse whinnied startled by the pistol's loud report.

"Did you hear all that up there, Sally?" shouted Koen towards the attic door. "When I've sent the golem out, I'm coming back for you!"

His curiosity piqued by the sound, Koen descended to the ground floor and peered through a crack between the warehouse doors to spy a group of men standing by a barrel laden cart across the road, which was strange for the building across the way, like most of the property at this end of St. Ada Row was empty. That was one of the reasons they had set up their base of operations here, that and the close proximity to the canal then one of them took a revolver from his pocket and broke open the chamber to check it was loaded. Koen cursed under his breath *they were police in workman's clothing.* He went to the golem and reading quickly through the Shem, tore off the beginning to leave only the instruction to kill anyone in its way. He re-rolled the parchment, stepped onto the short ladder and pushed it into the creature's mouth. It shuddered into life, the awful glittering eyes regarding him.

"There are people outside who are in the way, deal with them!" he ordered.

Sally descended quietly from the attic and stopped to regard Schul's body sadly then hearing the clump of the golem's footsteps, peered nervously over the first floor stair rail to see Koen below busily working on something and remembering what the old man had told her, crept quietly towards the rear staircase.

Chapter Twenty Seven – The Golem on St Ada Row

On hearing the shot, the policemen cautiously approached the warehouse doors only to be taken by surprise as the golem came crashing out. They fired their pistols to no avail as it stomped onward to dash them aside like ninepins, the giant even picked up one unlucky soul to throw him bodily at the few of his fellow officers who had fled.

Now the monstrous being was in plain sight Guthridge could see how close Parret's description of it was, at over ten feet tall it bore a striking resemblance to something a child might make of clay. Still blackened in places from the fire, its head was shaped like a mediaeval pot helm with glittering glassy balls for eyes and below them a slot-like mouth concealed the Shem.

Inspector Poulson was standing with the professor further up the road, with a firing party. "Get of the way, you idiots!" he shouted at the fleeing officers.

"Take steady aim, fire!" ordered Sergeant Thicke as the golem approached. A volley of rifle shots hit the steadily advancing figure slowing its progress slightly but the bullet damage quickly refilled itself with clay from within and thus renewed it continued trudging relentlessly towards them. "Fire at will!" he bellowed in amazement.

"Bloody hell, it's fixing itself as it goes!" exclaimed Poulson.

"You have to hit the mouth, that's where the Shem is!" shouted Guthridge over the din.

A khaki wagon pulled by a pair of horses had turned into the road and a uniformed figure jumped down to join them. "Lieutenant Poole at your service!" announced the soldier smartly.

"About bloody time!" the inspector snapped.

"Sorry, got held up by your blessed roadblock!" he answered by way of explanation. "Now if you bluebottles could just get out of the way?"

The wagon had been turned so its rear faced down the street and the tailboard was dropped to reveal a machine gun team manning the new model Maxim.

"Aim for the head and let the bloody thing have it!" ordered the officer and turning to Guthridge asked. "That's right isn't it Prof?"

Guthridge nodded and with a rat-a-tat the Maxim spewed a torrent of bullets at the golem's head shattering it into pieces, the written parchment of the Shem was shredded and the whole thing crumbled into a heap of clay fragments.

The obvious threat now gone, the police regrouped and were headed towards the warehouse when it was rocked by a tremendous explosion. "Oh my god, Sally might have been in there!" exclaimed Guthridge in shock as the building, now aflame, began falling in on itself.

"We had had better get back, Inspector, the buildings down here are so close together it's likely the whole blooming lot will catch fire!" suggested Sergeant Thicke to his superior.

"But, what about Miss Miller?" asked Poulson, the heat from the burning building was intense.

"Look, over there it's the woman!" cried a constable

pointing down the street and sure enough, there was Sally staggering out of an alleyway wrapped in a smoke-blackened blanket and clad in only her undergarments. Lieutenant Poole dashed forward to snatch up the young woman and carry her to safety as the entire row went up in flames then helping their injured comrades to safety the entire company retreated to Hilda Road to watch the conflagration.

Chapter Twenty Eight –
A Week Passes

When the blaze had finally abated and the fire brigade were able to douse the flames there was little left standing at the canal end of St Ada Row. A pair of charred skulls and several fragments of larger bone were recovered from the burnt remains of the warehouse, but of the second golem there was no sign. Sally Miller recounted how she had seen Koen busy with something before making her escape and from this Inspector Poulson surmised he had been killed while setting up a booby trap that had exploded prematurely. Satisfied the danger was over he released Rabbi *Goldman*, as he still insisted on calling himself, from protective custody. Professor Guthridge however, advised caution as the bones could not be positively identified but the policeman, under pressure from his superiors was eager to bring an end to tawdry newspaper headlines such as *"The Monster of Golders Green!"*

Sally Miller appeared to be every bit as tough as she portrayed herself but nonetheless was invited to Pendleberry Hall along with Evelyn, at Lady Mary's insistence, to recover from her ordeal. Lt. Poole insisted on accompanying them "to make sure that Sally was alright", Evie and Mary laughed at this, both knowing full well that Algy had taken a shine to the winsome actress. Guthridge meanwhile decided to stay in London for a few days to discuss the Kabala with Goldman while prevailing upon his friend the inspector, to remain vigilant.

A week later, after the fuss had died down, Rabbi Goldman was about to lock up the synagogue following the evening's Amidah while thinking about his former comrades. Aaron, Rudi, that bastard Ticho, all killed by Koen's lust for revenge, *which he himself had escaped thanks to the intervention of the Oxford Professor*. The Hand of God was no more and its thumb cut off but Goldman felt he would never find peace until he received forgiveness from the Lord himself.

Joseph Koen had by all accounts proved to be the animal he'd always imagined but on the other hand, Isaac Schul seemed to have possessed a surprising streak of humanity. Although Samuel was certain the man would still have killed him given half the chance.

A noise took his attention and he turned to see a hooded figure stood by the lectern. "I'm sorry but I've finished for the day" the figure did not move or speak so reluctantly the Rabbi stepped towards the stranger. "But if you have a problem, I suppose I could make time for you."

"You have no time left to make, Adler!" stated the figure in a familiar voice.

A shocked Goldman heard a heavy footfall behind him and turning to see what it was screamed in terror…

Chapter Twenty nine – Sidney's Discovery

Sidney Parret was standing at the top end of St Ada Row and something was troubling him, a week ago he had picked up nothing from his reading the site of the conflagration, this was not so unusual as meddling with the occult often seemed to muddy the waters as it were, so he decided to try again when the psychic fog had cleared.

The medium ducked under the temporary barrier and wandered down to the site of the warehouse to see several figures in dark blue uniforms picking through the charred ruin, one looked up as he approached. "Hello Sidney" said Sergeant Thicke.

"The Inspector got yer on cleaning duty, want to borrow me brush and dustpan?" joked Parret.

"Ha-ha very funny, Sid" replied Thicke. "My idea actually, something doesn't add up, we haven't found Koen's gun anywhere which I think odd. You'd expect it near where his bones were found and what about the other bloody golem thing? All that heat should have baked that clay solid but we haven't come across so much as a brick."

"They could have kept it somewhere else, on a boat

perhaps?" suggested Parret.

"We searched the boats as soon as the fire died down, nothing."

"Yeah it is funny that, things don't seem right to me neither."

"Spirits not talking to yer Sid?" shouted a constable who was sorting through the ash with a shovel. "Try a drop of the hard stuff, always makes my old dad see things what aren't there" several of the other policemen laughed, much to Thicke's annoyance.

"Gercha!" yelled Parret in response and leaving them to it, walked down to the towpath to stand looking over the water, the darkness of a week ago had receded but he could still feel an almost residual anguish, someone else had been brutally killed here recently.

The hairs on the back of his neck stood up. "Ello guvnor, been a funny old week ain't it?" said a voice by his ear.

Sidney turned to address its owner and smiled. "Well hello yourself, who are you then?"

* * *

"Bloody hell, I thought all this was over!" exclaimed Poulson in exasperation as he regarded the body of Samuel Goldman.

"It's just the same as the first one we found, sir" remarked the sergeant standing next to him. "Head's all stomped flat."

"Thank you for stating the obvious, Sergeant Burton!" he replied angrily. It was just as the sergeant had said, the man lay spread-eagled upon the floor as if he had fallen backwards enabling the golem to stamp on him, as if confirm this observation bloody footprints faded slowly away as they led to the synagogue door.

"Poor sod, must have seen it coming?" opined the sergeant. "Constable Brown found an eye under one the pews, must've popped right out!"

"I'd prefer you spare me the gory details in future Burton and locate our friend Mr. Parret." The professor had gone to Cambridge to attend an academic conference and was unavailable at the moment, *damn it Arnold I need your expertise.*

* * *

Now back at Scotland Yard Inspector Poulson slammed the telephone receiver down angrily, Guthridge still hadn't returned *and* the porter did not know where he was staying so he left a message for Arnold to call Scotland Yard immediately upon his return. *Damn it, Parret had confirmed Goldman had been killed by a golem but he could not ascertain who was controlling it, was there a third conspirator they did not know of?*

There was a knock at his office door. "Excuse me Inspector, but that *Parrot* bloke's here again" explained Sergeant Burton.

"Good, show him in!" ordered Poulson.

"S'cuse me Inspector but I've got something really important to tell you" Parret was clearly worried.

"Well Sidney what is it?" Inspector Poulson's face paled as the medium recounted what he had discovered on St Ada Row. He was about to call Burton back when the sergeant burst into the room with disturbing news, fingerprints taken at the synagogue matched those from Wallace's ledger and there was a report from a guard at Paddington Station, a man matching Koen's description had been seen overseeing the loading of a large crate onto a goods train. "Koen, when was this?" asked Poulson in alarm.

"Yesterday afternoon, sir" he replied.

"Where was the train bound?"

"Oxford."

"What? Find me the railway timetable!" then picking up the phone he demanded. "Connect me to the Oxford

Police, this minute!"

Parret made his excuses and left quickly, he had an important telegram to send.

Chapter Thirty – Instrument of Vengeance

While the fuse burned on his makeshift firebomb Koen exited from the very same door that Sally had used to escape only minutes before. He spotted the girl tottering down the alleyway in the direction of St Ada's and realised in that moment that his former comrade had deliberately left the attic door unlocked.

Furious at how he had been betrayed yet again Koen was considering shooting the actress in the back when a voice made him start. "Spare a penny for a cuppa guvnor?" it was a down-and out begging along the towpath. Koen angrily vented his anger on the unfortunate, viciously clubbing him to death with the butt of his pistol. Then he had an idea and after dragging the unfortunate man's corpse into the warehouse, he hurried to his boat to reach the vessel just as the building erupted in flame. *With any luck when they find his body they'll think it's mine.*

Koen had lain low for a week waiting for the dust to settle, then after dispatching Adler the golem had been crated and transported to Paddington Station where he personally supervised the loading of his precious cargo.

Upon reaching the university town he hired a cart and found refuge in a disused boathouse on Castle Mill Stream not far from his intended target's residence. As he sat patiently in the dark eating a meagre supper, Koen contemplated his strategy. *The Golmi was an instrument of vengeance, wasn't it?* It was time to get even with the man who had dared to meddle in his plans, the clever professor who had outwitted Schul.

CHAPTER THIRTY ONE – A GOLEM IN OXFORD

Alighting from the train, Evelyn ran from the station to her residence holding up her skirts to avoid tripping over them on the way and causing great consternation to the staid denizens of the university town while also garnering whistles from several students going to lectures. Once inside, Evelyn caught her breath then sought out her pistol from the bureau and after loading it left to proceed briskly towards St Aidan's, not running this time, *she would need a steady hand if came to shooting.* Evie nevertheless still managed to cause alarm as the sight of a woman of a certain age striding briskly along St Thomas Street, hatless and brandishing a Webley Service Revolver was not something one saw in Oxford every day.

A police constable stepped in front of this apparition to say. "Excuse me madam, you can't walk around the streets brandishing a gun."

"You bloody idiot, get out of my way!" shouted Evie in a most unladylike fashion.

The constable was nonplussed. "Madam, really I shall have to…"

Evelyn put her face close to his to snarl. "Professor

Arnold Guthridge of St Aidan's is in dire peril so if you want to do something useful, go find some of your fellows and start searching the college for him *and* make sure they're armed!" with that she strode on.

While staying at Pendleberry Hall, Mary, her niece had attempted to mesmerise Sally and after several attempts the actress remembered how the old man had put some kind of spell on her and that under its influence she had revealed everything including the plan to locate the second golem and also told how Professor Guthridge, realising how the conspirators located their prey, came up with the idea of frequently moving Adler about to keep him safe from detection. Koen was presumed to be dead so, believing the danger to be over, Evelyn decided to wait until her return to inform Arnold of this and gave it little thought until an urgent telegram arrived.

The message was from Parret and she read it with shaking hands. *"Urgent, Koen not dead, coming after Professor G. Sidney."* While at the canal side the clairvoyant had been approached by the spirit of the murdered down-and-out, who explained that Koen had used his body to throw the police off the scent and warned Sidney, *that the foreigner wot killed him was out to get the interfering clever bloke from Oxford.* Evelyn did not question the veracity of Sidney's warning and having been driven at speed to the local station in Lord Theddingworth's own coach, had boarded the first train to Oxford.

Upon reaching St Aidan's the astonished porter informed the formidable Miss Poole that the Professor, after returning to his quarters had taken himself off for a walk instructing the man, that, should Evelyn call he was to be informed immediately upon his return.

Evelyn racked her brain as to where Arnold would go then remembered how they often strolled along the banks of the River Cherwell behind Magdalen College. It was all she had to go on and informing the porter of her intention was on the point of setting out when Fenwick and Brigg arrived to offer their assistance, they had been walking through the quadrangle and had spotted the Professor's lady friend looking perturbed. Evie quickly told them of the golem and after acquiring an axe and a large crowbar from the groundsman's shed, the trio set off in the direction of the river.

Meanwhile Professor Guthridge, completely unaware of the danger he was in or how many sought him, was strolling along Addison's Walk enjoying the bucolic surroundings and musing on his relationship with Evelyn. She had been more affectionate of recent but Arnold, concerned that he might be reading more into it than he ought had stopped for a while to gaze absentmindedly at the swans swimming in the Cherwell when a heavy footfall broke his reverie and a long shadow was cast over him by the afternoon sun.

"Professor Guthridge, vengeance is come upon you!" said a voice in an accent redolent of Bohemia.

Guthridge turned in shock to see a tall clay figure there with a bearded man stood a little distance behind it. "So, this is the other Golmi therefore you must be Koen?"

The statuesque creation was a work of art, Wallace and Snodgrass being masters of their trade had fashioned it in the form of a Greek god of Herculean proportion giving it a distinguished noble face in which were set glittering glass balls for eyes.

"You are quite correct Professor Guthridge and now your time is come!" replied Koen.

"Then I assume Rabbi Goldman is no more?" asked Guthridge, desperate to stall the inevitable.

"Yes, my golem crushed his head like an eggshell, a fate you will share!" snarled the man.

"This is a new tactic is it not? Attacking me openly in the daytime, why not wait until night when it would less obvious?" he began backing away.

"I don't have time for delay because your clever friend the Inspector has set the Oxford police searching for me!" he gestured to the golem. "Enough stalling, kill him now!"

Guthridge did not wait for the monstrosity to carry out its instructions but ran as fast as he could. He was a senior member of the Aidan Harriers, often taking part in runs around the countryside and after seeing the original's performance on St Ada Row guessed it would not have a great turn of speed.

As he fled Guthridge heard Koen shouting after him in mocking tones. "You can run Professor but you will tire eventually, my golem will not stop until it has crushed the life out of you."

He could hear the steady tread of the clay giant falling away behind him but knew the truth of the man's words, he could not keep up this pace forever *there must be a way of stopping the damned thing!*

As he approached the bridge that led to a pleasant area known as the Grove, two policemen, stationed there as part of the alarm raised by Inspector Poulson lifted rifles to their shoulders. "Quickly sir, across here we'll stop the swine!" yelled one.

"No, run!" gasped Guthridge pausing briefly to catch his breath. "It just wants me don't stand in its way!"

"Don't you worry about that sir, we'll handle it" the officer reassured him.

The golem was getting closer so calling on the officers to flee once more, Guthridge set to running again, hearing several shots behind him followed by screams as the clay monster tore the officers apart. *Two more unnecessary deaths, Koen, you absolute bastard!*

Guthridge raced across the green making his way towards Longwall Street hearing people cry in terror as the clay giant pursued him. Running down the road he ducked down an alleyway only to find it led it into a long wide yard with several tall cast iron gates. Guthridge frantically tried each one in turn only to find they were all locked tight. There was no way out, *he was trapped!* As the plodding footsteps grew louder, Guthridge threw himself bodily against a sturdy door at the far end in a futile attempt to break it open then after draining his strength, turned and leaned against it to face his fate only to see that the creature had stopped a distance away. It appeared to be waiting, regarding him with its malevolent glassy stare, *why?*

Of course, Koen wanted to be there to see him die!

Chapter Thirty Two – Final Confrontation

The man in question entered the yard holding his side with a bloody hand, for a stray bullet fired by one of the unfortunate officers had wounded him. "You see Professor, you cannot escape me!" he boasted despite his pain. "Did you really think you could escape retribution? You really are a…" he didn't finish, as Cornelius Brigg, who played rugby for the college, arrived to lay him out with a mighty punch.

The determined trio had heard the shooting as they hurried along Addison Walk and after discovering the remains of the unfortunate policeman Fenwick had spotted Koen some distance away, limping across the Grove. The athletic Brigg gave pursuit immediately wielding the axe over his head like some mediaeval warrior with Evie lifting the hem of her skirts once again to run after him leaving Fenwick, the least athletic of the three to follow as best he could. The rugby player arrived first and after dealing with Koen began laying into the golem with the axe as Evie ducked under its swinging arms to join Guthridge who had sunk to the ground in exhaustion.

"Arnold my dear, are you alright?" asked Evelyn cradling him in her arms.

"Evie get out of here it only wants me!"

"Nonsense my love, I will not let it kill you!" she affirmed raising her Webley.

"You must shoot the Shem out of its mouth, it's the only way to stop it" he gasped feebly upon seeing her determination.

"Get out of the way Cornelius!" yelled Evie, loosing off a shot that hit the being in the head knocking out one of its glassy eyes.

Fenwick, now caught up, began swinging at the creature with the crowbar, hewing out chunks of clay only to see them be replaced from within.

"Move you idiots!" screamed Evie to no avail.

"It keeps healing itself!" cried Fenwick before being dashed to the ground where he lay unmoving.

Brigg dashed to the front to bury the axe in its chest but the golem knocked him backwards with a single blow and began its clomping advance once more.

Her line of fire was now clear and Evie, holding her right hand steady with the other sighted along the barrel of her pistol to fire three shots in rapid succession. This time her aim was true, one bullet loosened its jaw, a second went wide but the last took it clean off, the Shem fell out to flutter to the floor and the clay giant froze in its tracks.

"Good shooting Miss Poole, I thought you dead but it seems I was wrong?" Koen had regained his feet and was pointing his revolver towards the couple at the far end of the yard. Evie pointed her weapon again and he laughed. "Here we are just like before and you with only two bullets left, you know you can't win this game against me don't you?" he taunted before cocking the pistol.

Brigg had regained his feet and stumbled dazedly against the immobile golem which, being of superior workmanship to the first, had not broken into fragments as before and now toppled backwards in one complete piece to fall upon Koen with all its weight, crushing his head in an echo of the fate he had brought to the members of the Hand.

"Bloody hell, did I do that?" asked the burly student before falling unconscious once more.

Poulson turned up a scarce five minutes later with Inspector Nichols, his counterpart in Oxford and a horde of armed officers in tow.

Chapter Thirty three – Guthridge calls on Evie once more

Young Fenwick was admitted to hospital with a broken arm and a fractured tibia, Brigg on the other hand, was made of sterner stuff and had suffered little more than cuts, bruises and a slight concussion. After we had given our statements to Nichols and Poulson at the local police station Evie and I retired to my study at St Aidan's where we talked late into the night until we both fell asleep in the large leather chairs. Nothing untoward happened between us and Evelyn left bright and early in the morning leaving instruction that I was to visit her later.

Evie had informed me that her brother Algy and Sally Miller have struck up quite nicely but it did make me feel sorry for poor Cornelius and David who were both quite sweet on the actress.

Furthermore, I have to admit that this business with the golem has re-ignited my thirst for the paranormal and have decided to dispense with my exposing of fraudulent psychics (this will no doubt be of great relief to Madame

Hecate and her ilk) to concentrate on investigating unexplained phenomena once again.

So it is with that I close this latest tale in my journal, I will shortly be setting out to call on my beloved Evelyn and I confess to holding great hope that soon we may be properly reconciled.

A. Guthridge (Professor of Arcane Studies, St Aidan's)

That evening, the professor, arriving at Evie's house a full quarter hour earlier than suggested paused uncertainly on the steps up to her front door and hearing the music of a sitar coming from her front parlour knew instantly what it meant. The blinds were not fully down and peeping under the scalloped net of the bay window he saw Evie performing her yogic exercise to the sound of a gramophone record, naked as nature intended. Guthridge furtively watched as she moved gracefully, admiring the curve of her back and the swell of her bosom. Evie had permitted him to watch her exercises many times before and remembering what it was usually a precursor to, thought on what it was like to feel those fine thighs around his waist. An image of those legs clasped around Bumstead sprang into his mind to spoil the memory but surprisingly did not dampen the ardour that had arisen as he played Peeping Tom to Evie's Godiva. The professor was then taken by surprise as she raised her head to look straight at him and smile, unsure of what to do he retreated down to street level hearing the sitar music stop abruptly.

The front door flew open and there stood his beloved wearing only the thin red silk robe he always admired her in. "Arnold, I wondered where you had got to?" she asked

"Erm?" was all he could say.

"Come back up here this minute!" she ordered and he meekly obeyed, her face was flushed with a delicate sheen upon it and her dark blonde hair was loose about her shoulders once again. The robe was gaping at the neck barely covering her ample cleavage and the heady aroma of patchouli hung about her.

"Evie, I didn't intend to pry" his heart was racing *what must she think of me?*

"I knew you would arrive early you old silly, it was my intent that you should see me thus and I must admit I found it quite exciting" she admitted with a grin.

"Oh er, I don't know what to say?"

Evelyn took his hand. "Arnold Guthridge you are such a fool, come in and make sure you shut the door behind you!"

Other titles by BLKDOG Publishing that you may enjoy:

Sirkkusaga
By Kyt Wright

A saga — a long story of heroic achievement, especially a medieval prose narrative in Old Norse or a long, involved story, account, or series of incidents often named for the principal character.

Several hundred years after a world-shattering war, two of the surviving nations, the Reignweald and the Dominion, have fought themselves to a standstill, both remaining determined to control of what's left of it.

Sirki Vigsdottir, a songstress who performs under the name Freya in folk-rock group *The Harvest*, is a beautiful, self-centered woman who is fond of drink and a recovering addict to boot — not the sort of girl a boy brings home to Mother.

Following an attack from an unexpected quarter, abilities awaken within Sirki, who begins a journey of self-discovery. These new-found skills attract the attention of both the Psi, a mysterious group of telepaths headed by the fearsome Mina and an equally sinister government department – the ACG.

Sirki, learning the real truth of her origin, is dragged into plotting between the queen and the Government, finding herself in constant danger as Bren, fighting for the nation, becomes an important part of her life. As it becomes clear that her life of self-indulgence is over, Sirki wonders if her new-found powers are a blessing or a curse.

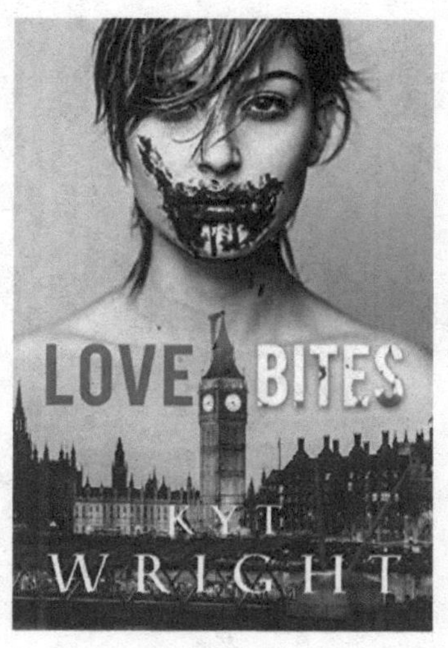

Love Bites
By Kyt Wright

Elisabeth Bathory wears a police uniform and patrols the streets of London at night.

Elisabeth Bathory is over four hundred and sixty years old.

Elisabeth Bathory is a vampire.

Elisabeth Bathory enforces the Edict ensuring humans are never killed by vampires.

Humans are starting to turn up dead and it's obvious her people are behind it!

Arthur: Shadow of a God
By Richard Denham

King Arthur has fascinated the Western world for over a thousand years and yet we still know nothing more about him now than we did then. Layer upon layer of heroics and exploits have been piled upon him to the point where history, legend and myth have become hopelessly entangled.

In recent years, there has been a sort of scholarly consensus that 'the once and future king' was clearly some sort of Romano-British warlord, heroically stemming the tide of wave after wave of Saxon invaders after the end of Roman rule. But surprisingly, and no matter how much we enjoy this narrative, there is actually next-to-nothing solid to support this theory except the wishful thinking of understandably bitter contemporaries. The sources and scholarship used to support the 'real Arthur' are as much tentative guesswork and pushing 'evidence' to the extreme to fit in with this version as anything involving magic swords, wizards and dragons. Even Archaeology remains silent. Arthur is, and always has been, the square peg that refuses to fit neatly into the historians round hole.

Arthur: Shadow of a God gives a fascinating overview of Britain's lost hero and casts a light over an often-overlooked and somewhat inconvenient truth; Arthur was almost certainly not a man at all, but a god. He is linked inextricably to the world of Celtic folklore and Druidic traditions. Whereas tyrants like Nero and Caligula were men who fancied themselves gods; is it not possible that Arthur was a god we have turned into a man? Perhaps then there is a truth here. Arthur, 'The King under the Mountain'; sleeping until his return will never return, after all, because he doesn't need to. Arthur the god never left in the first place and remains as popular today as he ever was. His legend echoes in stories, films and games that are every bit as imaginative and fanciful as that which the minds of talented bards such as Taliesin and Aneirin came up with when the mists of the 'dark ages' still swirled over Britain – and perhaps that is a good thing after all, most at home in the imaginations of children and adults alike – being the Arthur his believers want him to be.

A Storm of Magic
By Ashley Laino

Being brought back from the dead is an impressive trick, even for magician Darien Burron. Now he must try and use his sleight of hand to swindle modern-day witch, Mirah, to sign her power away, or end up a tormented demon in the afterlife.

Meanwhile, sixteen-year-old Mirah is starting to lose control of her powers. After an incident at her aunt's Witchery store, Mirah is sent to a secret coven to learn to control her abilities. While away, Mirah meets up with a soft-spoken clairvoyant, a brazen storm witch, and the creator of dark magic itself. The young woman must learn to trust in herself before she loses herself entirely to the darkness that hunts her.

silent. Arthur is, and always has been, the square peg that refuses to fit neatly into the historians round hole.

Arthur: Shadow of a God gives a fascinating overview of Britain's lost hero and casts a light over an often-overlooked and somewhat inconvenient truth; Arthur was almost certainly not a man at all, but a god. He is linked inextricably to the world of Celtic folklore and Druidic traditions. Whereas tyrants like Nero and Caligula were men who fancied themselves gods; is it not possible that Arthur was a god we have turned into a man? Perhaps then there is a truth here. Arthur, 'The King under the Mountain'; sleeping until his return will never return, after all, because he doesn't need to. Arthur the god never left in the first place and remains as popular today as he ever was. His legend echoes in stories, films and games that are every bit as imaginative and fanciful as that which the minds of talented bards such as Taliesin and Aneirin came up with when the mists of the 'dark ages' still swirled over Britain – and perhaps that is a good thing after all, most at home in the imaginations of children and adults alike – being the Arthur his believers want him to be.

A Storm of Magic
By Ashley Laino

Being brought back from the dead is an impressive trick, even for magician Darien Burron. Now he must try and use his sleight of hand to swindle modern-day witch, Mirah, to sign her power away, or end up a tormented demon in the afterlife.

Meanwhile, sixteen-year-old Mirah is starting to lose control of her powers. After an incident at her aunt's Witchery store, Mirah is sent to a secret coven to learn to control her abilities. While away, Mirah meets up with a soft-spoken clairvoyant, a brazen storm witch, and the creator of dark magic itself. The young woman must learn to trust in herself before she loses herself entirely to the darkness that hunts her.

Weirder War Two
By Richard Denham & Michael Jecks

Did a Warner Bros. cartoon prophesize the use of the atom bomb? Did the Allies really plan to use stink bombs on the enemy? Why did the Nazis make their own version of Titanic and why were polar bear photographs appearing throughout Europe?

The Second World War was the bloodiest of all wars. Mass armies of men trudged, flew or rode from battlefields as far away as North Africa to central Europe, from India to Burma, from the Philippines to the borders of Japan. It saw the first aircraft carrier sea battle, and the indiscriminate use of terror against civilian populations in ways not seen since the Thirty Years War. Nuclear and incendiary bombs erased entire cities. V weapons brought new horror from the skies: the V1 with their hideous grumbling engines, the V2 with sudden, unexpected death. People were systematically starved: in Britain food had to be rationed because of the stranglehold of U-Boats, while in Holland the German blockage of food and fuel saw 30,000 die of starvation in the winter of 1944/5. It was a catastrophe for millions.

At a time of such enormous crisis, scientists sought ever more inventive weapons, or devices to help halt the war. Civilians were involved as never before, with women taking up new trades, proving themselves as capable as their male predecessors whether in the factories or the fields.

The stories in this book are of courage, of ingenuity, of hilarity in some cases, or of great sadness, but they are all thought-provoking - and rather weird. So whether you are interested in the last Polish cavalry charge, the Blackout Ripper, Dada, or Ghandi's attempt to stop the bloodshed, welcome to the Weirder War Two!

Click Bait
By Gillian Philip

A funny joke's a funny joke. Eddie Doolan doesn't think twice about adapting it to fit a tragic local news story and posting it on social media.

It's less of a joke when his drunken post goes viral. It stops being funny altogether when Eddie ends up jobless, friendless and ostracized by the whole town of Langburn. This isn't how he wanted to achieve fame.

Under siege from the press, and facing charges not just for the joke but for a history of abusive behavior on the internet, Eddie grows increasingly paranoid and desperate. The only people still speaking to him are Crow, a neglected kid who relies on Eddie for food and company, and Sid, the local gamekeeper's granddaughter. It's Sid who offers Eddie a refuge and an understanding ear.

But she also offers him an illegal shotgun - and as Eddie's life spirals downwards, and his efforts at redemption are thwarted at every turn, the gun starts to look like the answer to all his problems.

Burning Bridges
By Chris Bedell

They've always said that three's a crowd...

24-year-old Sasha didn't anticipate her identical twin Riley killing herself upon their reconciliation after years of estrangement. But Sasha senses an opportunity and assumes Riley's identity so she can escape her old life.

Playing Riley isn't without complications, though. Riley's had a strained relationship with her wife and stepson so Sasha must do whatever she can to make her newfound family love and accept her. If Sasha's arrangement ends, then she'll have nothing protecting her from her past. However, when one of Sasha's former clients tracks her down, Sasha must choose between her new life and the only person who cared about her.

But things are about to become even more complicated, as a third sister, Katrina, enters the scene...

Click Bait
By Gillian Philip

A funny joke's a funny joke. Eddie Doolan doesn't think twice about adapting it to fit a tragic local news story and posting it on social media.

It's less of a joke when his drunken post goes viral. It stops being funny altogether when Eddie ends up jobless, friendless and ostracized by the whole town of Langburn. This isn't how he wanted to achieve fame.

Under siege from the press, and facing charges not just for the joke but for a history of abusive behavior on the internet, Eddie grows increasingly paranoid and desperate. The only people still speaking to him are Crow, a neglected kid who relies on Eddie for food and company, and Sid, the local gamekeeper's granddaughter. It's Sid who offers Eddie a refuge and an understanding ear.

But she also offers him an illegal shotgun - and as Eddie's life spirals downwards, and his efforts at redemption are thwarted at every turn, the gun starts to look like the answer to all his problems.

Burning Bridges
By Chris Bedell

They've always said that three's a crowd...

24-year-old Sasha didn't anticipate her identical twin Riley killing herself upon their reconciliation after years of estrangement. But Sasha senses an opportunity and assumes Riley's identity so she can escape her old life.

Playing Riley isn't without complications, though. Riley's had a strained relationship with her wife and stepson so Sasha must do whatever she can to make her newfound family love and accept her. If Sasha's arrangement ends, then she'll have nothing protecting her from her past. However, when one of Sasha's former clients tracks her down, Sasha must choose between her new life and the only person who cared about her.

But things are about to become even more complicated, as a third sister, Katrina, enters the scene...

**Father of Storms
By Dean Jones**

Imagine losing everything you loved as well as the future you'd wished for so long to come true.

Seth was born with the gift to manipulate energy. Unfortunately his skills mark him as a target for one who wishes to control everything. So began a life running from those who would seek to command him, a life that spans over a thousand years waiting for the day when all will be once again as it was.

Captured in modern day London, Seth needs the help of his companions, the Mara, to show him who he is through dreams of his past, so he can save the family he has waited so long to have. A warrior bred for battle must fight once more – but this time the battlefield is his mind. Can Seth win, or will he finally lose who he is and become the weapon of the man who started his nightmare all those years ago? *Father of Storms* is a story told through time, a tale of love and hope where there seems to be none.

BLKDOG

www.blkdogpublishing.com

www.ingramcontent.com/pod-product-compliance
Lightning Source LLC
Chambersburg PA
CBHW011922050726
47591CB00007B/2291